# A Slice of the Watermelon Moon

# A Slice of the Watermelon Moon

## a novel

Daniel Wesley Williams

*for*

The real "August" because of all those great nights.
Craig Rowland because you were always there.
Neil "Dutch" Mutchler Ibarra because of your camaraderie.
Leigh Almond because you listened.
John Brunner because you never let me down.

*Those, who think they know,*
*know not.*
*Those, who know they do not know,*
*know.*
—Spiritual Text

# *August*

He was a big man with broad shoulders and a tan, along with a little bit of a belly, but nothing that detracted from his masculine beauty. A little devious and a bit of a liar, but these little things were only present for the benefit of others. He was very generous with his work-a-day wealth. I'd say very solid and a hard worker. Younger than his years, he liked to have a good time and drink beer. A good person, but he only doled out a compliment if he thought it was going to enhance the moment. To receive his rare approval was a joy and made you feel quite special. Secrets and guilt, maybe a legacy passed down from his Jewish mother, or maybe just remnants from the road; he was a trucker after all was said and done. I think he still loved his ex-wife, but one couldn't tell. They shared a daughter and a history, that's for sure. She was a harsh, hard woman, who grew up on a dirt floor with snow pouring in on the West Virginia nights. He had the opposite—a nice big house, loads of pot, and a 305 Super Hawk Honda. He drank beer with his mother; I think she encouraged his creativity.

This is only a sketch, an outline. Who could really tell what went on under that beard? His ex was equally as mysterious, sharp to the teeth, with dark eyes. Hatred was there as well, plus a distrust of anything unfamiliar. It was like what the cat dragged in—everything was unfamiliar from her perspective. He didn't like the word, but he was a gypsy of sorts, a colorful smart man, edgy and funny, maybe a little fearful of death, but wholly unwarranted. He had a strong heart and meaty country hands. He was a little bit salty, but in a dirt road kind of way. Not to say he wasn't sophisticated, he was, sold recliners by the side of the road for god's sake, jewelry too. Always knew how to make money, should have been rich, he'd tell you, missed some opportunities. Her fault, he'd say, she didn't see the light. One couldn't blame her. She grew up poor, had to fight for every meal, a risk was a risk, ready to snatch security from her mouth, food as well. She never drank; her father had done enough of that, making corn liquor by the side of the house. She was explosive, rough and rude. She burned like vapors from the still.

My childhood was explosive too. During my time in middle school and high school, I contracted cancer of the buttocks twelve times from the toilet seat in the student bathroom, and I also had a bout of hoof and mouth disease, from the little fat boy who kissed me in the back of a U-Haul truck his father was driving. I experimented orally with him on a trip to the small town of Saint Mary's Georgia, and this developed into a certain death sentence, since his crotch had some kind of musky odor, which I thought to be most definitely the thing that was killing all the gay people at the time.

I knew I was a gay person because my older brother always called me gay. He wasn't being mean or even trying to tease me; he just said it as a matter of solid fact. I remember looking at myself in the mirror and saying, "You're gay, and at least you won't have to worry about getting some girl pregnant." I kept this as my personal business for years!

I'm Cecil and I now live in a brown, nineteenth century, double shotgun house on Rocksprings Street in Athens, Georgia. It has a thin front porch with two wooden porch swings. It is cold in the winter and hot in the summer. There is tin covering the steep roof, and when it rains, I can hear the raindrops hitting it like quarters. This is not comforting like people say, but frightening. It sounds like mortar shells landing above me. I have woken up screaming many times. I have had snakes and chipmunks invading my rooms for years, but the worst thing is the damn squirrel that comes in through the cracks and eats the fringe off my Iranian rugs. I would blow his little head off if I could catch him, but I don't keep a gun in the house for fear of blowing off my own. My house is haunted and that's what possessed me to start traveling south, in search of sun and someone.

I met August on the road and that was the start of a kind of naughty secret, just like I had at our small private school. I followed his truck down the highway and flashed him. To my surprise, he waved for me to go ahead. We met at a motel bar. I was nervous, but August was calm. We had a couple of drinks and agreed to meet again. Later on that month, I drove down to Ocala to see him. I got to the motel lounge a little early, chit-chatted with the bartender, and grabbed a table near the karaoke stage. It was one of those old guest lounges with faded carpet and green vinyl chairs. My new friend tiptoed in a few minutes later and massaged my shoulders before he sat down.

"I thought you wouldn't come," said August.

"I had to, wouldn't miss seeing you!" I said.

"Where you been this week?"

"Had to go to Miami. It was a light load, not too much trouble. Traffic wasn't too bad either. You want a beer?"

"Sure I'll take one!" I said.

I lit a cigarette and thanked god this was a smoking bar. I had thought about quitting but the nicotine eased my nerves.

Our conversation was mundane at first, but I could tell August wasn't ordinary. There was a richness about his very presence that was at once down to earth and mysterious. He appeared to have a cloud about him that was dense and intelligent. His looks matched—dark hair cropped close and drunken hazel eyes, the kind that blinked as if through a pool of water. It was apparent that August was very comfortable in his own skin, so different to what I felt.

"Have you ever been to West Virginia?" August asked. "I grew up near Bluefield,

West Virginia. I was born and raised in a valley north of Bluefield."

"Just once, I was on a trip to Pennsylvania and we stopped at a place called the golden palace, kind of a Hare Krishna Hindu temple in the middle of nowhere."

"Well, if you're not busy next week, you can go with me," August said. "I have to go up there and it should be pretty this time of year."

"Yeah I'd totally love to go; I don't have anything else to do!" I replied.

Not to appear too anxious, I straightened my shirt collar and took a drag from my Marlboro.

"We'll meet at my house and go from there," August said.

The bar was beginning to get packed, and the waitress came over to ask if we would like to hear some music and have another cocktail. We both ordered a beer. Some guy in a cut off t-shirt got up and did a country number. August winked at me, then strutted to the dance floor and started to slide around in his cowboy boots. I started smiling and clapping my hands, feeling better than I had in months. He finally came back to our table, slapped my back, and said, "See ya later."

I spent the next few days wondering about this man I had just met. Was he an ok kinda guy? He was certainly gorgeous, but was he safe to be around? I had done this little trick with truckers before and always had the same thought: they could be very dangerous! This was the first time it had gone past the fantasy I had developed. I couldn't believe I had followed him into the motel parking lot, much less had a cold beer with him. The one thing that kept me sane was the easy way he had handled me. The invitation to West Virginia had been a shock, but it did not shock me badly enough not to do it. My attraction for him had taken control, and I was going to take the risk.

I got to August's cabin a little early the day we were to leave. I found that he had left me a note saying that the house key was under a turtle shell on his outdoor deck table. I let myself in and casually snooped around the great room. The walls were covered in tongue and groove pinewood, and the floors were made out of thick planks stained red. He had his air conditioner going and it was frigid and crisply inviting. The kitchen area was all handmade and wooden, with a large antique rake on top of the cabinets. I really had not expected his place to be so nice and cozy. When he had told me that his cabin was in Grayberry, I almost had a fit. My longtime partner lived in the same area. This part of Georgia was growing out of control and many out of state people had moved there over the last two decades. My trucker man finally drove in the yard, greeted me with a rough grunt, and immediately said to load up.

The trip up to West Virginia was long. August seemed to be somewhat detached as he navigated the highways. He would later tell me, some years after, that driving his truck was meditative, but also fun. He would sometimes make prank phone calls to local police departments and medical establishments. When he first told me about this, I thought it was very funny. But whenever he would talk about West Virginia, it would bring up thoughts of his ex-wife Agnes. He always started the story the same way: he's a twenty-two-year-old bartender and Agnes walks in the bar with long black hair dragging the floor. She sits at the bar and nurses a Stroh's beer through a straw. He fell in love with her instantly. In his mind, that was his first memory of Agnes. She, of course, had another story.

I was not quite sure I myself believed in love at first sight, nor was I aware of what this dark man sitting next to me was thinking, but I was well aware that he was a platinum rewards club member at the Holiday Inn motel, and that was exactly where we were headed. As we exited the interstate, my body was flooded with endorphins. I was not sure how this little interaction would proceed, but the blood was pumping furiously through my modest heart. August suggested we buy a bottle of gin before we checked in, and I thought this was an absolutely great idea—some kind of greedy relief!

He seemed so calm, like he had half expected and done this many times before. I was later to learn that indeed he had done it many times before, but only with women. I was the only man, or so he said. Bluefield, West Virginia, was called the air-conditioned city, as it was situated in a high-altitude area of the state, and indeed August possessed the very coolness of the mountain air, and the very handheld cold slickness of a piece of coal. August had spent much of his twenties in the Bluefield area, and Agnes, his ex, was raised not far from this town. In its heyday, Bluefield had been a center of commerce and a bustling mining town, but it was now in decline. August said that the decline had reached a zenith with the collapse of the old Matz Hotel. One day as he was walking along a street downtown, he heard a cracking sound. As it happened, the foundation of the once quite grand hotel had been sinking for years and the noise he heard was the beginning of the fall of the facade. It fell only five feet from where he was standing, nearly crushing him to death. Lucky then, and still lucky now, he said.

I had been lucky too, but for different reasons. I had suffered for over fourteen years with bouts of depression and psychotic episodes, sometimes having to be hospitalized close to suicide. My luck was from the fact that I never followed through with my thoughts, and somehow came through the darkness. I had a wonderful time with August during that trip. Oftentimes it was a nail-biter—I still had it in my mind that he was going to turn mean on me. This never happened, and we, or at least I, had some of the best sex in my life! Eight weeks went by: I would go back and forth from Athens to Grayberry. I met his ex-wife during this time and August and I got to know each other better. Soon I crawled back into the cab of his Ken-worth. He had been gone on a trip to south Florida, from Miami across the Tamiami Trail to the wealthy town of Naples, and back to Georgia. He had worked on his tan and was three shades darker. I, on the other hand, had been trying to land a job, with no luck and a lot of stress!

This was, however, a clear and beautiful morning in Georgia, and we were headed north to Virginia. I had never been to Virginia, and knew nothing of it, but August assured me it was beautiful. As we were riding toward Richmond, I had an insight. I had fallen in love with August probably the first time we met! It was under sort of sketchy circumstances, but no worse than people meeting in some trashy bar! One thing that bothered me immensely was his take-me-or-leave-me attitude. He had been on the road for so many years and alone for such a long time that he reminded me of a cowboy, one that had been on the round-up and in the weather and dryness for a lifetime. He scared me more than a little. Agnes admitted to me one night that she was frightened by August too. She was a hell-raiser and a rough woman, and could definitely take care of herself, so this was a surprise to me. The moment she uttered it, I understood immediately. I think something passed between us then, as it would many times after. She had no idea that August and I were having an affair, and would probably tear my head off if she did, but she did know I considered him special.

"You seemed to be out of it!" August said.

"I'm just worried about not having a job. It's been a long time, and nothing seems to be improving."

I had been going absolutely crazy the past two years because of my situation, and in fact had worried myself into a drinking habit. August had the effect of a nice smooth blanket on my worries. For some reason, I always felt relatively happy around him. I had two descriptions in my mind for August: one was the serene beauty and the other was the sea captain. When he was clean-shaven, head and face, he had an intense look—that's when I called him the serene beauty. When he would grow his big curly goatee, I called him the sea captain. He had no idea I had these names for him, and I'm sure he would call me crazy, but these descriptions were fitting. Agnes told me he had two personalities, and I was beginning to recognize them myself.

We talked non-stop the whole way to Richmond. My man was pulling things out of my head left and right. I was in the mood for hearing his stories too. He had a real manly way of treating me, but it was laced with a little feminine guile.

This recognition reminded me of the fact that I was born without a father. For thirty-three years, the entire length of my parents' marriage, and many years before that, my father was a slave. His days and nights were completely controlled by the hot summer sun and October moon that so violently rose and set in my grandfather's eyes. He had two faces too. One face had a family and the other face had only the planting and harvest. My mother tried her heart out to be the good woman behind the man, but my father was a transparent being, like a featherless bird chirping for more crumbs from its cold, mindless mother.

August told me he didn't have a father either; he was born not long after his death. His mother was excommunicated from her wealthy family mainly because she married a gentile and also because she became poor. She was unable to take care of him so he was raised by his benevolent grandmother, an old woman living in the valley between two West Virginia mountains. August was secretive and hardly mentioned anything about this fact. He only said that his grandmother took very good care of him, and that she was a woman of means. He told me they owned a few cows and raised a bunch of chickens, and he spent his time riding his Honda bike every day and living in the big old farmhouse; he was rich nonetheless.

He had an intense feminine side that he inherited from his grand. This feminine side was part of his dual personality, which was only apparent to people that really paid attention, or people that loved and cared for him. I, by now, had become both of those. Agnes, even though they had been divorced for years, was one of these people as well, but she seemed to be blinded to his real nature, as were most women. He could slip in and out of a conversation like a chameleon, and in and out of a room so fast it would make your head spin. Agnes was the first one to pick up on these changes, and it always made her so angry. I was more forgiving. I wanted him to pay attention to me, and I wanted to be close to him. Being in love with a man like him was being a fish in an angler's lake; the man would get you on the hook but then suddenly break off.

I showed up out of the blue and uninvited one weekend. August did not take too kindly to this. He was afraid that the hunters next door would somehow suspect that he and I were having an affair. Months into our affiliation, August also seemed to have taken on a female companion. I called her God-awful Girdy. I was beginning to realize that August was not what he appeared to be. One day he would be very loving, and the next day he would be very dismissive. He was very concerned with what people in the surrounding area thought of him. I could not blame him. He lived in a rural area, and the people that surrounded him seemed to be very judgmental. It had taken me awhile to get it in my head that this man was going to break my heart. Essentially, this was nothing new to me. I had, for many years, walked around with much anxiety and fear. Sadness always accompanied these feelings. I was not sure exactly what I was in love with: a mind, a body, or a fiction in my head. If it was fiction, it was no less than the one August presented to others.

August had a particular scent. He always smelled of oaken campfire smoke and toasted almonds. I don't think the smell had anything to do with real almonds—it could have been the soap Agnes used when she washed all of his clothes, or just the bar of soap he washed himself with, but anyway, I could pick up on it fifty feet away. I had not realized at this point how intoxicating it was to me, or how difficult it would be to stay away from him. We didn't see each other for a while, nor even speak for a time. I thought of him often, and finally he called. He had such a pleasing personality and giving nature that I forgave him immediately. He also asked me if I would like to go on another trip with him, this time to Indiana. The fiction that was August did not extend to his kindness toward me or the tactile and extra sensory explosion I felt for him. I was very excited about this trip, and I think he was too. We were scheduled to go on a Sunday, but the day before, he was standing around the campfire and took off his pants. He threw them into the fire and didn't realize his wallet was in the pocket. We had to postpone until the next week, and this had me on pins and needles. By my very nature, I knew that I wanted more than just a few trips with August. I knew that somehow, deep down, I was trying to open the cabinet of his heart. By his very nature, I knew that this was a virtual impossibility. Nonetheless, we sat on August's porch, he looking altogether like the handsome sea captain, and I looking altogether like the green-eyed German that I am. We were waiting for the sun to rise, but right then the melon moon was shining.

August had a lot of work to do that week, and I always loved to see him on the tractor hauling wood or building a bonfire. He was a person that never stopped *doing*. He had massive muscular legs, and a hard curved back that was smooth and sexy, covered in dark skin and no hair, all developed from hard work. I will not say that our relationship was purely physical, although this exciting fact came into play often. August was indeed a very handsome and appealing person, but I was mostly interested in his personality and keen, sharp sense of humor. It was astounding to me every time I thought about it. August was raised in one of the most rural and backward areas of the United States, but years on the road and interactions with all different sorts of individuals had heightened his mental attitudes and behavior. I almost felt, even though I was an urban person, that he was somehow more socially sophisticated than anyone I knew.

The next week started with a great relief. After much haranguing and trouble, August's driver's license was finally granted. We again hopped into the cab of his big truck and were off. A change was evident in his demeanor. I think it had worried him immensely that he had been sidelined from his job. After all his complaints about being on the road and working all the time, I think he was actually addicted to the excitement that the road offered him, not to mention the money, of which he always seemed to have plenty.

"I was just thinking of you, the moment we got into this damn truck," August said.

"You know, how we met was funny! If you hadn't been so crazy at the time, and I hadn't been so curious, this wouldn't be happening."

I had thought about it as well, and had an insight. It was surprising how people could meet in such a way as to be all cock and balls one day, and then the next day become very honest with each other. I especially was guilty of this. August had been fairly honest from the get go as well, a little mysterious, but essentially truthful. His weathered face and hands told a story, even if he didn't. Right then, I spoke very slowly.

"I was so nervous the first time we met, you had no idea. For all I knew, you could have been some kind of horrible, dangerous man."

"I would never have hurt you," he said.

"Yes, but I didn't know that."

I sat there, doe-eyed, wondering what this square-headed man was really thinking about me. I knew that I had somehow risked my life. He knew it too, but I could honestly say it had been worth it. As for him, I suspected he would keep up his distance and only let me in on intimate occasions. I knew I was pissing up his left leg and I also knew he was some sort of alien to me. From the beginning of our time together, to the present of our quirky and clandestine relationship, my affection for him was undiminished.

# *Agnes*

"**D**amn you, August, I had the best of you!" Agnes yelled. Then she pivoted toward me.

"Cecil, for twenty-five years, we were married and I had the best of that son of a bitch!"

It was a Saturday night and we were all sitting around the kitchen table in the cabin. As usual, Agnes was seething, spouting something awful about her ex-husband and, in her opinion, criminal and chief conspirator in her miserable life.

"He's slept with every woman on this road! His nails are as black as night!"

I had my doubts about what she usually said concerning this, but it was a question in my paranoid mind. Grayson Farm Road certainly had its share of scandalous and single women. There was Ashton, the local horse-raising farm girl, and her sister Gayle. Gayle had committed suicide two years earlier after a cocaine infused biker party, and Ashton was known to wander through the neighboring hunting camp completely naked, except for a pair of riding boots and a cowboy hat. Their uncle had been a graduate of MIT and a notorious businessman-slash-womanizer. This had given the whole family somewhat of a moneyed cache and charm. I wondered if this fact had attracted August.

Agnes's sprayed, feathered mullet was bobbing up and down, and I knew she had more to say. Her vitriol was always surprising; it was like she was burning from the inside out. She had

had a hard life, that's for sure, but August had provided for her during their marriage, and they still had a strong connection that seemed to endure. "Don't sit across this table with a smirk on your face, I know what you are!" Agnes whispered. I had a whisper in my head too, but for the life of me, I didn't know what August was.

"You're an asshole, August, and a son of a bitch! Your mother hated me! She didn't think I was good enough for you!" Agnes's voice was rising.

"Don't let him fool you, Cecil, his family had plenty of money, and he's not so innocent either! I remember the first time we met. He knocked on my apartment door, announced his name, and walked right on in!" She snickered. "I said to myself right then and there, this man is trouble!" Agnes shook her head from side to side, mullet following.

August's hazel eyes glazed over and he poured himself another Maker's Mark and ginger. For him, this was years ago, but for Agnes, it was always as if it was just yesterday. She longed for West Virginia. The Georgia heat, in all of its incarnations, had not been that kind to her. She was always in a state of near vexation. She believed in the fear of God, but also in giving him a good cussing at the same time. The big black boot was going to fall in her presence at any moment! She thought it was going to land on August, but it usually fell on her. This appeared to be the essence of her fortitude and mountain-holler hardness. Her departure for the mountain state was imminent. I wondered if she would ever actually leave Georgia and and go back to the dirt floor. I also wondered if it might somehow be better for her if she did. As it happened, Agnes had gone almost completely blind at the time. This was so disturbing for August and I because she had been such a hard worker. Now she was unable to do the most simple of tasks. Of course, this did not include the task of lambasting August. She was an expert at this, and no pesky eyesight problem was going to deter her.

# Old Truckers and the Great White Hunter

"Hell, Cecil, cain't you wear something normal!" August shouted through the barn.

Just for the hell of it, I was wearing white linen pants and my handmade Mexican sandals. I guess this outfit was just a little too queer for Mr. Kammer, even though it was 100 degrees and the sun was melting the tar on his black fence. We were preparing for a visit from his trucker co-workers and the owner of the land across the road. He was getting nervous. August wanted me there, but I wasn't sure exactly why.

The morning passed, and it was time for his friends to arrive with their beer coolers and packages of frozen ground deer meat. I snapped back at him for a minute and then continued to set the buffet table by the washhouse. August was placing wood in the fire pit so as the night came on, we could have a small fire. These guys expected a party, so that's what we intended to do—give them a great big shindig!

I had met the landowner a few weeks before, and Possum described him as the "Great White Hunter." I understood why dear Possum said this, because when he spent the night at the cabin, he wore loose boxer shorts that gave me a peek at his very white balls, which flopped through the fly.

The trucker guys were a mystery though, and this was August's main concern. I made everything picture perfect. The buffet was loaded with crawfish, corn, chips and dip, and my own Southern fried pork chops. I even made a nice Magnolia flower arrangement in an old pickle jar, and August said it was pretty. He finished up the fire pit and we waited on the steps of the barn.

"You know, you're going to have to calm yourself down," August said.

"Don't rub my head or be too sweet."

I knew that as the party went on and he got bored with the guests, he would want me to give him some attention. I overlooked the sweet part and told him I would, by no means, rub his head. I could wait for when we turned the nightlight on and got into bed for that. He hopped off the step, rubbed my shoulders, and said, "Thanks for your help."

The first vehicle to drive up was the land-owner. He limped in on his old four-wheeler and got off in front of the barn. He was wearing an old raggedy hat and a camouflage jump suit with green Army boots. He had a bottle of bourbon with him and placed it on my buffet table. He stated that he was starving, so I directed him to the chips and dip.

The next group to come through the gate was headed by Marvin, one of August's co-workers. The load that got out of the Ford truck was surprising—some were old, some younger than me. All were dressed in some form of camouflage, plaid, or Wrangler jeans. Marvin approached lightly, wearing what looked to be dirty blue jean shorts and an eighties concert t-shirt. I closed my eyes for a second and imagined I was in the Bahamas.

August was thrilled, I could tell, but he kept cutting his hazel eyes over at me, as if I was going to suddenly haul out the rainbow flag. Other cars and trucks started to come in and the yard became full.

## A Slice of the Watermelon Moon

The hunter had parked his little old camper in August's front green area, and he was planning on spending the night there. After the last person arrived, we all walked down to the fire pit. August paid little attention to me as he stoked the glowing wood. He got on his high horse, proclaiming that no one should have to take a drug test, then proceeded to pass a big fat joint around the crowd. I took one hit and walked back up to my buffet. The hunter guy followed me and ran into his camper. He whistled at me for a second and I could guess what he wanted. I kinda wanted to do it, but I fixed the drinks and ignored his calls. His whistling was pretty though. He did the whippoorwill and this always reminded me of my childhood. I imagined him sitting on the hard, cheap upholstered couch, pale white balls shining. Later, I regretted not seeing him, but I knew August would be next to me as the moon came out, and the evening faded.

August turned on his satellite radio station and turned it to an old country music show. One of the guys took his shirt off and I caught Mr. Kammer looking at him. This was the first time I ever saw him appreciate someone's masculinity. The man was hot, I will admit, so I guess he couldn't help himself. This little private moment sent electricity through me instantly.

The men seemed to be enjoying themselves, and August was having a blast. I decided to fix everyone a shot of cold moonshine and saltine crackers with pimento cheese; I didn't want anyone to vomit up the shine. August's friend down the dirt road made the liquor and it was strong.

After the shot, Marvin inched up to me, and ever-so-slowly tapped his boot on the big granite rock by the bonfire.

"How do you know this son of a bitch?"

"We've worked together for years and I've never seen you!"

The one hit of pot was still working on my brain so I just cackled and grabbed my crotch. He sort of got my meaning, so my heart went *thump-thump*, and I asked him if he would like another shot of moonshine.

"Yeah, buddy, gimme one," he said.

"Alright, you want some juice with it or just straight?" I asked.

"Nothing straight around this place, and juice is fine!" he grunted.

Marvin took to me just fine after that, and we talked the night away.

August got sloshed and fell into the fire a couple of times. His boots were burned, but he got out without a scar. All my delicious food was consumed by the truckers, and the hunter passed out early in his camper. There were a few stragglers that didn't want to leave, but we led them up the yard and into their respective trucks. The party had been a success!

I held August's hand as we walked back down to the cabin. He seemed to be pleased, but melancholy. He stripped off his jeans and t-shirt and drawers. We sat at the kitchen table for a few minutes and ate some leftovers. I could sense that he was still wanting to party, but I went into the bedroom, got under the covers, and said goodnight. August came into the room later and wrapped his big legs around me, our bodies entwined for the duration of the night.

# The Melon Moon

We approached the stuffed black owl with the red plastic eyes perched on August's fence; it was used as a deterrent for deer. That night, we had taken the four-wheeler across the road to look at the huge silver moon. August was talking in riddles, and this scared me to the point of paranoia. The owl looked to me to be some kind of dried and feathered voodoo totem. I mentioned this to August, but he said he was all out of omens. He thought the horse was out of the barn about our relationship, and I had never seen him appear so weak. It was as if I were talking to a tanned and lotioned bag of flesh. He appeared to be drooping! If it hadn't been for his strong and curved back, I would not have recognized him. I had not, at this point, realized the gravity of his situation. Time would tell, but had I not learned to live in the now? I really tried to impart this fact on him, but it seemed to fall on old ears, the kind of ears that were not accustomed to hearing this sort of information.

"I don't give a damn what these people around here think of me!" I said. "The only thing my father ever taught me was to not care what people say. But I am only a tourist here, and this is something that affects you, so I do care for your sake. Anyway, what the hell could these people do? Burn a cross in your yard? I don't think anything like that would ever happen to you, August! All your trucker buddies are pretty cool, they've travelled a lot, and I'll bet you a million dollars that some of em have done the same damn thing we have."

My tirade went on.

"It's much worse to just flat out lie. People can see through that in a minute. I'm sorry I brought this on you, but I'm not sorry for anything we've done. Plus, what the hell do you think goes on in these hunting camps? You think they don't fool around, you're fucking crazy. Anyway, no one knows for sure what we do."

I adored him, but my words were sad and frantic. He blustered that he didn't care either, and they could all fuck off. I knew deep in my heart that this was a fissure as large as the Grand Canyon we planned to visit in his namesake month. I left that morning, after the fabulous moon, with a great fear. For three days, I prayed to the nonexistent god for help. On the third day, August called. In my little decrepit head, I had won. I was never sure, and one can never be, what he was really thinking, but his smooth voice drove me to the point of elation. The melon moon had been a powerful aphrodisiac, but I never imagined it would taste so sweet.

The days after this went by fairly uneventfully. August began walking several miles each morning, and I began to write more. Then, a new situation emerged. August was suddenly no longer a truck driver. He had been fired from his job. This was the first time I had seen him have little to do. God-awful Girdy was no longer in the picture either. Her lover had moved up from Florida. Girdy and her husband lived in the house, the boyfriend landing in the camper outback. I was not sure how this retirement would affect him, but he seemed to be pleased. Girdy's new boyfriend was a little jealous of August, but I was glad she had someone in her life.

August had always been a pot smoker and was enjoying his

new freedom. He would close the farm gate in the evening and sit on the porch with his stone pipe. His sense of humor was so apparent when he would smoke. I loved to sit there with him and rock in the rocking chairs, make snide comments and dancing to his new satellite radio station. August had managed to save quite a bit of money and had ended up moderately wealthy. He still referred to Agnes as a dream killer, and blamed her for him not having what he should have had. Although he was twenty years older than me, he still seemed to have a dream in his head. I wondered what it really was, and I was going to find out even if it killed me...or at the very least turned me into a nosey bastard. There was something in August's background he was hesitant to tell me. I couldn't understand if he was being cagey or if there was something that he was hiding. He really didn't have to worry what he said to me; I had dropped my defenses long ago. He could have told me anything and it wouldn't have quelled my softly-directed Southern warmth. I will admit that he didn't quite understand my Southern nature, and it is a particular nature that only a few people have experienced at my age. I have always said that I was raised centuries in the past and there was only one person that I could truly relate to on this level. It was almost as if I were a foreigner in my own time. August would entertain the thought and call me quite a man, but he really didn't have a clue about what really entertained my mind and gave me my sense of humor. He had his own sense of history, and we usually played on this. This was enough for me. I didn't expect that he would somehow suddenly realize I was truly a rebel at heart. I do not try to present myself as a novelty, but it did happen occasionally with August. He would usually dismiss it instantly, to my chagrin. He possessed a certain masculine quaintness, and it peeked through more and more during our lazy days on the porch.

I was, however, running into a little problem with our ex-tended time together. Mostly it was August's problem. One theme that was evident in our association was the fact that he liked women and men. I tried my best to see what side of the road he fell on. I always questioned whether or not he could actually love a man. Standing on the porch steps one drunken evening, he stated that he could not. I was not sure if this was a statement about me personally or if he was really saying never ever. I hoped it was a mental block that could be overcome, for indeed I had allowed myself to continue thinking of him as a lover. If I could not have all of him, as that seemed to be impos-sible, at the very least we could have a great affair. I asked myself, why this man, and why at this time during my life? I was no spring chicken and neither was he. He had a whole helluva lot of baggage, and I was not the most stable person. The one thing I could say was if there had to be baggage, at least it was going to be Louis Vuitton. More fitting for August, it would probably be alligator skin. He was tough by anyone's standards and I think this is what attracted me to him. I was tough too but also very sensitive. If I could have him just a little, and if he would give just a bit, I would be pleasantly surprised!

# My Southern Nature

I remember my first friends. They were the children of the men and women who for generations had lived and worked on our farm. It was not a large plantation like one would see on film, but rather a small family farm of about five hundred and forty acres. It is situated on the outskirts of the Chattahoochee Valley in southwest Georgia, and is in my father's name still to this day. These facts have contributed greatly to the way I interact with most people, including August. I am by all accounts a bastard child. My mother, at the age of twenty-three, had an affair with a tattooed and arrogant navy man. I was the unwelcome and red-headed product of their secret encounters. To foreign ears, this may sound like a Southern cliché, but to me it is more than real. It almost permeates my very being, seeping into everything that I do. I suppose that I matched August's West Virginia weirdness point for point, although he was much more stable and balanced in many aspects…most, in fact.

The moment I graduated from college, I flew to Europe, Germany to be exact. There, I had a wonderful time with great German friends and explored the western part of Germany and France. It was one of the most memorable times in my life. I had somewhat of a love affair with a tall, handsome, blonde, German man, and was almost the toast of his ancient and lovely town. After my tour of Europe, I returned to the United States and lived in Manhattan. I worked in a small art gallery on the upper west side. The shop was owned by a tiny Chinese American woman, and we catered to the very wealthy and semi-famous. The one thing I remember about being in New York was that it was very hot. I lived with a composer and actor couple, and we could not afford air-conditioning. I stayed there several months and then returned to Georgia. Five months later, I had my first psychotic episode and was trapped on the red dirt road.

I have, all of my life, had relationships with dirt roads, but this one is special. It runs directly through our family land and connects us to reality. At this time, however, it connected me to a fantasy in my head.

When I began to be psychotic, the smell of burning black candles in my nose was very strong. I imagined that the witches down the road were casting a spell, and I was their subject. The voices were getting louder as well. It was like ten thousand evil people screaming in my head, crescendo after crescendo of piercing terror. My mother, being the staunchly religious person that she is, promptly took me to every known exorcist in South Georgia, including, but not least, a black preacher, who if not by supernatural means but rather his own loud voice was going to scare the devil out of me. I ran screaming out of his church, formed my own deluded opinion, and checked myself into the psych ward of a local hospital. To the left, the muddy dirt road had delivered me to the old-time religion, to the right, it had delivered me to modern science. The gravel-topped Grayson Farm Road delivered me to the dark skinned, sparkling, hazel-eyed August. There are only a few houses on Grayson Farm, and the road is winding with many hills that were impossible to navigate. During a rainstorm, its red mud bubbles up through the gravel and becomes slick. It is beautiful but treacherous. The hardwoods and pines mingle together to form a tunnel along the way and this keeps it cool during the hot summer.

In contrast to this shaded and lovely dirt road, there was one that led me to a mystery. That was the pitted and dusty road called Boiling Creek. My biological father Van resided on this short and miserable stretch of desert. He lived in a gray, two bedroom, ram-shackle old shack. It was my daddy's big mouth that I heard first—since he was blabbing to every convenience store clerk near the farm that I was not his real son—but it was my mother's indiscretion that would lead me to this little corner of Georgia, and the corner in my mind that was overrun with fear and errant, unknown DNA.

The moment I met Van, it was fire! His life was tangled, mixed up with the Masonic order and endless glasses of rum and coke. His gray shack still held the ghost of his long dead second wife, and the ghost of his unhappy dead son, and the daughter with whom my daddy had had such an illegal attraction. The first thing he told me was that during his navy days, one of his dear shipmates had been in love with him, and that he did not care that I was a homosexual, he understood completely! He would later tell me that his beloved shipmate blew his head off because my father, being a masculine man, did not return his love! This was the first indication of my genetic makeup and my mother's holy contempt! I was a Mason's son and would always be protected, he said. Indeed, he conjured up one of his Masonic brothers to give me my first intense sexual experience! The big, hairy man was to come to the porch of his shack and penetrate me. During this psychotic episode, I had come up with the delusional idea that if some man were to penetrate me, the voices would subside. I'm sure Freud would have much to say about my delusions, but he probably would be a little too clinical about the situation. I thought then that the hirsute Mason brother would be a good catalyst for my transition into a free individual. The whole idea appealed to me on a base level, but as the man was approaching, and the dogs were barking, the plan was foiled by my nosey mother's unexpected intrusion. My experience had to wait, but it did not have to wait too long.

One thing about being Southern and having my particular taste was the fact that there was no shortage of Wrangler-wearing cowboys that captured my attention! None was more evident than the neighboring farm's felonious, tractor driving, blond-headed hunk of a man named Oliver. Oliver had crooked white teeth and, like the August, was a bisexual man. But unlike August, he did not see his dual role in nature as detrimental. He was as wild and free as anyone could possibly be. He approached me first and we carried on for many months. After a while, his criminal mind took over and he was sent to prison and taken from me. Due to this loss, I was hospitalized a few months later. After being in the ward for a while, I regained my medicated composure, drove to Macon Georgia, and there, at a tattoo parlor and esoteric bookstore, I met Possum.

Possum had a bald head, beautiful sea foam blue eyes and size nine feet. He was standing behind the glass counter in the store, and greeted me with a twangy old-style Southern accent and a completely open mind! His open mind, I would later learn, was just like a sponge, soaking up everything and forgetting nothing. He was like an open photo album—look what we did here, look what we did there! The first night we met, I went home with him immediately. His home, like my biological father's, was a gray shack in the middle of the woods. Upon seeing this hovel, I had fears that he might in fact kill me later on, but these fears were quelled when I found out that he was as sweet as an overripe Georgia peach with a Kentucky drawl.

I am a Georgia peach, and Possum is a Georgia peach—Elberta to be exact. The Elberta peach is a delicious cash crop for the great state of Georgia. It has a rosy red, fuzzy complexion and is dripping with sweetness with just a bit of tartness at the end. If my meaning is misunderstood, it is with good measure. We did not know at the time that we were related, third cousins specifically. It seems the universe had conspired to bring us together, and not only give us a glorious time, but also to lead me to as yet unknown branches of my family. As many spiritual gurus claim, a coincidence is nothing more than angels that coincide. In my opinion, God is not a benevolent entity sitting in space, but a conspirator using cause and effect to slam us into the very next moment. There was something sacred about Possum, and all of our moments were memorable for us both. He was, and is, my hairy, jockstrap wearing, Unitarian cohort of the cast iron skillet and woven peach basket.

# Soft Heart

I fall somewhere between an artist, a business minded person, and a paranoiac. I think because August was a father, he knew this about me. I have never been a successful person in the work sense, but I also have never been tied down either. August had been treated rather cruelly by Agnes and used by many people. This was something that I never ever intended to do to him, and I created a space in my frugal head to hold this notion. I was aware that August was himself a hard man, and could be called cruel in his own way, but he did always try to treat me with some respect.

All of life is sorrowful, as the Buddha says, and this sorrow followed him in such a subtle way that it was hardly noticeable. He always seemed to be, if not happy, at least very solid and stable. This was my dark and lovely time-bomb of a man, although the fuse was very long, and most probably wet. He had to have a saturated wick with Agnes; she was no still small voice in the corner, but rather an agitated container of diesel fuel. I knew that he somehow led her on, and he probably did this with me as well, but he did it in such a way as to always be above us lower individuals. If any other person had tried this tactic, it would have been condescending, August always pulled it off like a bank robbery. He did know on occasions that he had been caught by me, but these were rare and could only have been thought of as humorous glitches. He was a blue tailed, striped sand sister people thought was poisonous, but in fact was so vibrantly colored that most were just astounded and knew to keep their distance. I enjoyed this colorful aspect of him immensely, as well as the more volatile side of Agnes. They certainly were a pair, one that had spent a lifetime together.

One afternoon, we were sitting at the kitchen table and August peered over his reading glasses at me, his kaleidoscope eyes flashing. I had never caught that kind of look from him before. I knew that he was going to tell me something important and something that was bothering him. I became nervous and stared right back. What was coming would take me aback, but my spine was stiff and I resigned myself to his thoughts.

"What do you want with and old man like me?"

He slammed the refrigerator door, marched outside to the front deck, and sat in his grandmother's old metal chair. Walking closely behind him, I was thinking that this was some kind of subterfuge. Certainly he knew this had never once disturbed me, even in the slightest. Whether someone had said something to him, or our time apart had changed his attitude toward me, I didn't know.

"I always want to be friends with you, Cecil, but I have to change my lifestyle."

The fact that he still thought of us having sex as a "lifestyle" was astounding. He was just not from the generation that had modern ideas and scientific backing in this regard. His understanding was so backward as to be almost comical. Of course, this did not make his words any less hurtful, for I knew that this time, he meant what he was saying. The religious guilt and societal pressures were just too much for this country man.

"Have you never enjoyed our intimacy?" I questioned.

"That doesn't matter; I'm just not comfortable with the situation anymore." He snorted. "We have to keep our friendship separate, and I don't know if you can do that."

Those few words he uttered then would have me reeling for days. It did not matter that later that evening as darkness fell, he would invite me to his bed. The fissure that had occurred on the moon-filled night had only gotten larger. August was wrong, however; I definitely could keep things separate. What he did not and could not realize was that I would walk through a burning inferno for him. What I had seen, shining from his eyes, was not a cold hard shard of ice, but the blazing blue and green incandescent fire of his mountain heart.

# Stars

The dream was one of a series, and the last thing I heard before I awoke was this sentence set to music: "The stars follow all the wonderment in the sky and the moon stands in its place." The sun was in its place at that time, though, and I was staring into August's bearded and wet face. He tended to be a big slobberer when he slept, and the drool would moisten the creases of his mouth. It was not unusual for me to wipe his lips mid-conversation, since it would also happen when he got excited during a party or when he had had a few drinks. I would also rub his feet every time I saw him. This was to make him feel good, and also to keep the circulation going in his extremities since he was a diabetic and loved his libations. I cannot rightly say why I did this for him, or what he really thought about it, but I will say that during our hours together, he was very sweet to me, and his conflict was somehow diminished in the private way of looking at things. I was going to leave all avenues to my heart open. I had no clue whether or not he would continue to show himself to me, but I was definitely going to be there for him. In fact, I had always felt that Agnes was the only one who held the sacred skeleton key to his center being. She had certainly had the time and energy to grasp August tightly for many years. Her fist was so strongly clinched that I sometimes felt it would strangle the life and will out of him. She was my friend, however, and had come to my defense on many occasions. This knowledge did not make me feel guilty as maybe it should have. I saw her as someone that would be there for August if he needed help, and I knew that he would never even dream of restarting what her ignorance had torn apart so many years ago. The stars I saw in Agnes's eyes were love for him, but also real and metaphorical cataracts no amount of reasoning would remove! She needed to work on herself in the present, and stop working August over for things he had done in a murky, blind past life!

Agnes and I were sitting in the jungle, or at least, this is what I called it. In actuality, it is a concrete slab connected to August's nineteenth century barn. He keeps his big motorcycles there and it has been the scene of many a wild night. To my right the curious grey cat was playing with a leaf and to my left was the curious Agnes. August had gone to the cabin to retrieve a little green leaf. He had put on some music that had caused me to cry, and this had piqued Agnes' attention. I was the one that had a certifiable heightened awareness, but Agnes was just plain paranoid. She thought it was common sense, and it was in some degree, but to me it was mean nosiness and just one of her ways of scaring people.

She was a creaking bundle of walking sticks. Her tiny wrists and hands could manipulate August, and anyone that got in her way. Her voice showed her harshness and anger. August came back up from the cabin carrying the illegal load. He had been gone for a little longer than expected, and already smelled like the marijuana.

"Cecil, you want some of this?" He twisted the top of the pot jar open.

"I remember the last time you smoked!" Agnes said, warning me.

She was chomping at the bit, I knew, to get me into some kind of state where she could interrogate me. I had just returned from Hawaii and had smoked some fabulous Maui-Wowi, so I thought I would let the green genie do its magic and throw caution to the wind. August handed me the glass pipe I had brought him back from Oahu and seconds later, *whamo*, I was flying! Agnes did not partake, of-course. She always had to stay on her pedestal, looking down her dirt floor nose at what she perceived to be reptiles. That intense Georgia music August had playing, the subtle humidity, and the ghost of August's mother, whom Agnes hated, were on my side. At that point, I felt very protective of him, full of a blazing heat that would burn anyone that attacked him. This woman was pulling my leg, as she did August's, but right then, as things happened, she was stepping out of her league. Friend or not, she was abrasive, and always had been. Now, I will not say that this did not worry me. Agnes and August were dependent on each other, and she offered him some kind of home-sick balance. He had few relatives in either Georgia or West Virginia, and though he claimed not to miss his state, the fact that he still let Agnes in made it apparent to me that he held on to memories and ruts of his youth.

Tears streamed down both sides of my face. August was saying some kinda buddy-buddy bullshit, and Agnes was staring me down. The grey cat had stopped playing with the leaf, he started making comments about the thorny vine that was growing up between us. My daddy called this vine bamboo, although it is not. I think he associated it with the Asian plant because it grows so quickly, and can be a massive nuisance. This certainly foreshadowed my relationship with Agnes and her attitude toward me. The music was getting louder, and I wondered if he had picked it just to see how I would react. August treated others the same way his daughter and Agnes treated him: with mean sentimentality and cruel timing. This was the one thing that made me cringe in his presence. August exited the jungle, and Agnes and I followed through the barn, out to where the boat was parked. I staggered through the dense Georgia pines, not aware that this was going to be some kind of awful situation, but that's how it turned out. We sat down at the kitchen table, Agnes seething and I somewhat oblivious to her real intentions.

"Just what the hell is going on between you and August? Don't lie to me; I know you're having sex with him!" She was almost desperate.

In that instant, my mind collapsed. I am not a good liar but I was going to have to give it a shot.

"Come on, Agnes, we're just friends. He's my drinking buddy and really my best friend. That's crazy!" I think I sort of screeched it— anyone with a brain would know I was lying, but not about the best friend part.

This did add a little bit of truth to my words. August just sat there, like a big blob. He did manage to pipe up and give a little snort. *Damn,* I thought, everyone else suspected it long ago, I cared for her! She didn't have to be the last to figure it out.

"He's having sex with that other whore Girdy too—I know that for a fact!"

I couldn't believe she was thinking of me as a whore. I had had so little sex with so few people that I was practically a virgin. I always felt like a teenager with August—he was my soft and cuddly bear, and a seasoned love-maker. I was a grown-up kid lovin' a big trucker daddy!

"You're both gonna burn in hell, but I don't really care!"

Raising his voice slightly, August told me to say goodnight. I had been dismissed. He never addressed Agnes directly and left me feeling sick and paranoid. During Agnes's outbursts, I felt so sorry for August. Surely he didn't really have to put up with this kind of treatment! They were divorced—that was that. What hold did she have on him, and why did he appear so afraid of her? Her tongue was sharp, indeed, but he was slippery too and could always throw her out. I had thought that their codependency could only go so far, but I was wrong, as I had been so many times in the past. She just trudged along and seemed to win August over. He later drove me to Possum's shack, crushing what was left of the night. I walked down the hill to Possum's place and quietly opened the metal door.

"Why are you back so early?" Possum croaked, lounging on the sofa.

"I've been banished again, and I think Agnes knows about August and I."

Possum laughed, as he always did. He seemed to know the beginning and end of my stories before I ever told them. I could always count on him to bring me back to reality, and also add a bit more humor to the situation at hand.

Humor is exactly what I needed at that moment, and I wasn't so sure about the reality part, but that is what I was getting. Up until then, I had not really said, only hinted, at how cold August could be. It was always shocking when he turned frosty, since he had an A+ number one personality and knew how to entertain. Everyone loved him, and I mean *everyone*. The contrast between the lovable August and the loner August was frightening. He seemed to know exactly how to tighten the vice grip he had on my heart. Us Georgia people tended to bitch and moan, beating around the bush, trying to be cordial. The mountain man would let it be known that there was a nuclear explosion just around the corner, and you better get the hell away.

# Miss Pearly's Fried Chicken

I was a red-haired devil. That is how Miss Pearly described me during a conversation I had with her fifteen years ago. I remembered her vividly from when I was a child. She was employed by my family as a housekeeper and caretaker. Miss Pearly and Wes, her husband, would drive my brother and I back and forth on the farm road from my mother's up to her house on the northern end of the land. She would let us sit at the high leather bar stools in the kitchen and fry up anything my daddy had shot during the day. Her favorites, of course, were the chickens my family slaughtered during the winter—this was a luxury for all of us. I called her that evening during an intense psychotic episode. I was trying to get some information concerning my childhood and I was desperate to get in contact with some of the people who had lived on our farm. I cannot recall exactly why I was so interested in this. It certainly didn't help that she proclaimed me to be a devil, but it did give me some sort of comfort knowing she was still around, still wearing her gigantic straw hat, still fishing in the pond, and still frying up some of the best salty and crispy chicken I had ever had.

August did not have an even remotely similar childhood. He spent much of his time at the truck stop part of his family owned, stealing cigarettes from the machine and playing pinball. I garnered this information from him late one evening. It was something he was very reluctant to talk about. This left much room for me to fantasize, and much room for conjecture. I wondered if he had thought of the truckers as heroes or if they had been male role models. His nature was, in my mind, split between his grandmother's farm and her natural femininity, and the testosterone-infused swagger of the truck stop in Bluefield.

I thought of my childhood as compared to August's, and how it led me to him. We were opposites in many ways, and our age difference didn't help the situation. The one thing we had in common was a sort of fair-minded love for one another. I couldn't put my finger on it, but the few similarities we had made all the difference. He belonged in Nashville, and was his own celebrity. He had mentioned writing country songs several times, and I caught him with a writing pad stuck to his ass one evening—he was trying to hide it from me. He fumbled with it a second or two, and then let it drop out of his jeans. I was thrilled! I knew it had something to do with his dreams, I hoped he would let it evolve. The truckers he had known when he was a boy were all famous for something, all masculine peacocks strutting around, begging to be noticed, and they most definitely were by a young August!

I had always been attracted to the kind of man who might be a truck driver. I enjoyed looking at that kind of masculinity, the tight jeans, cowboy boots, and maybe a beard. My more urban friends always said I was entranced by the serial killer look. I think it had something to do with the men I use to see on our farm. They were not just regular guys, but men that were dripping with sex, hard workers, you know, and men with a purpose. Oliver's masculinity had been contrived, Possum's was over the top, but August had the whole package. If anyone ever said they wanted their birthday delight, with him, they could have their cake and eat it too.

Did any of this matter to August, and did it have anything to do with our friendship? I think it did! We had both been rather precocious as young kids, and he had garnered much attention as a football player and all around good guy. He had had a stint, during his youth, in Ohio. In that area. they are well known for their Cincinnati chili and their sexy corn-fed Midwestern boys. August still had childhood friends that would remember him from the football field and greet him in the local bar. From a gay point of view, I always said, well yes. Those sexy legs were still turning heads!

I was remembered by my longtime friends too. Every year, I threw a Kentucky Derby party at my mother's house, betting included. We were kids and didn't have much access to booze, so I would mix a noxious cocktail of cooking sherry and a bottle of whiskey my father used when he had the flu. It was an annual event that everyone looked forward to, and we still talk about it to this day. Miss Pearly was there, cooking up something delicious in the kitchen. Her husband was out in my father's garden picking beans, and my parents left us alone for the afternoon to be as wild as we were likely to be!

As of late, it seemed I would never know the real August, only the little snippets he deemed important. Some of these threads were from his childhood, and some were from his teenage years. He always wanted to keep it secret that he had a bit of Yankee in him. Honestly, if he hadn't, I would never have been attracted to him. I liked the edge he possessed and the snobbery he had with some of the people that would visit him. Because I liked this directness, Girdy even had the nerve to say I wasn't Southern. Little did she know, I was snooping around in her crush's past. Maybe I was delusional, looking for something that wasn't there or maybe, just maybe, I had found the soft underbelly that I knew in my steely little heart was ever-present!

The steel that I had in my heart was cultivated by another

woman on our farm, her name was Odessa. When I was a little boy, I would go down to the shotgun houses and play with all of the worker's children. Odessa was mother to two kids my age, Terry and Amy, and we always seemed to have a good time. We were just children back then, but what Odessa did would affect me and August down the road. That's because she taught me how to read bones. She would saunter out of one of the front doors of her tar paper covered shotgun shack, throw a bunch of twigs on the ground, and tell us kids to look at them. Every little minute curve or leaf was a human face. We usually did this to the sound of the vinyl record *Color by Numbers* by Culture Club and the faint background buzz of a cartoon Terry and I always liked to watch. She could tell whether someone was an honest person, crook, or if nothing else matched, just some kind of foreigner. August would have fit into this last category, for more reasons than just the shape of his face. Odessa knew her stuff, and I knew it too. I loved these differences and subtleties; they were at the center of my relationship with this exuberant character. Miss Odessa, however, did not tell us kids what to do if there was a foreign face shining back at us. I could always gauge the person through her eyes, but August was constantly surprising me, ripping my snobbery up and throwing it to the ground.

As far as August's soft underbelly went, I do not mean to say that he was shady or sketchy in any way, and my steely little heart is not mean! We were both just wary of how people viewed us, August especially. I was always concerned about being seen as transparent, and August always threw up some kind of near exotic aura around him. I personally witnessed him do this many times with people. It was like he was trying to say, *yes, I am packing heat, but I'm your best friend too and don't forget it.* I really don't understand why he never wanted anyone to know he was bisexual, except for fear of their judgment. Bi people certainly have the best of both worlds. I think he would have done well to maybe let it slip somehow; when people did find out, it did not hurt him. It had no bearing on his type of masculinity. Miss Pearly would have loved the guy, since she adored strong men. It was just a shame that I couldn't have them meet, but August would never have agreed to that confrontation!

# *Not Again!*

I picked up my smart phone, pressed August's name, and listened to it ring.

"Hello?" His voice was gruff.

I cringed, but managed to be cordial. I knew he didn't want to talk to me. I always felt like such a horrible nuisance when I called. In fact, I had begun to constantly feel like a heel when I talked to him. I don't think it was anything I was necessarily doing that gave rise to this, except the fact that I was seeing him every Saturday. I suspected Agnes had been at work on him, and I also suspected that because it was hunting season, he wanted to keep me away.

"Whatcha doin?"

"I'm sweeping out the barn." I could tell he was getting more irritated by the second.

"Just callin to see what you're up to," I said.

"Not much, just cleaning up and chopping wood."

Every winter, he would go up the road and gather logs for the bonfire. Lately, I would go over to find him fixing a fire just for himself. He would also be sitting in the barn alone, listening to music.

"You know nothing goes on around here," he said.

"August, everything goes on around there. You always have something to do."

"Yes, well, I haven't done it yet, but I am going to wash my hands of you." He was talking through his teeth now. "You coming over every weekend has gotten old."

"That hurts my feelings." I was breathless— it felt like he had grabbed my heart!

"I don't care," he said.

My mind went adrift then, and he muttered that he should keep his mouth shut. I think he'd had a few drinks.

"A steel tongue makes a wise head," I said. "Also, there is an old Buddhist thought that says, 'If your mouth was as quiet as your nose, you would avoid a lot of trouble.'"

I was no longer touching the ground. I should not have said either one of those things; all he wanted was a little privacy. He was an intriguing, older, a loner...and I was just lonely.

"Hmm!" he uttered.

"Well, I'll let you go." I was crushed.

For now, I could let him go from this phone call, but could I let him go forever, or even an extended length of time? The phone went dead. I couldn't call him back to say I was sorry, but that's what I should have done: told him I would respect his wishes and just fade away. I felt like this is what he wanted, for me to simply disappear. It was horrible when August cut me down like this; it was like a weight had descended on my very being. I think it was indicative of how much I cared for him. If he could treat me this way, surely my obsessive-compulsive head understood that he didn't love me at all...or maybe he did. That was the mystery of having a chronic mental illness. Sometimes, you can't tell reality from fiction, or your ass from a hole in the ground, as my daddy would have put it!

August didn't quite know it, but he had lost his youth. He may have felt it just a little, but what he didn't realize was that he had developed a certain gravitational pull by virtue of his age and experience. This was what so attracted me to him, but it was also what gave him a great deal of detachment. I was shouldering a whole helluva lot of weight, and I could imagine him walking around, just carrying on as if nothing could really get to him. I was quite certain that he was better off!

I dreamed of him from that day on, dreamed of him lying naked next to me, covered in his grandmother's old, heavy quilts, and me rubbing his sore neck and tanned shoulders. Lately he was going to bed with his little tight white briefs on, and I would have to tell him he didn't need these damn things, and slowly pull them from his body. I dreamed of this, the way only a crazy person would. My concern was that he would never allow it to happen again, and this pushed me into despair.

When I fall into the depths of my illness, my paranoid brain is set on an unending loop, and I see and hear things that aren't actually there. That night, I stood on my porch and saw the silhouette of a man. He was standing with his foot propped up on a tree, and he was wearing a black cowboy hat just like August. Olive, an old homeless woman, rode by on her decorated bicycle, and as the wheels were turning, I heard them say, "Forget him, forget him, we know, we know." I turned on the porch light because I knew it was a hallucination. I was aware that my love for August had been hinted at by others, others who weren't already "in the know". Girdy asked me if he might swing my way, as she often described it. I denied it vehemently. I knew that if I ever uttered the words, *yes, he does*, she would never speak to August or me again, and would cause trouble in the county. It seemed by virtue of his feelings that I had taken on the act of deception myself. I secretly hoped that one day, when I spent the night making love to him, one of these people would look through his bedroom window and catch us. Maybe, I thought, it would free him. More than likely, he would be mortified and be left with no plausible defense, causing tremendous guilt and outright fear.

This guilt that I was sure was bubbling up did not transfer to the bed, however. He would strip out of his cowboy boots and tight blue jeans so fast, I felt he would stumble onto his polished pine floors. This confused me at first, this lack of balance, until I realized that he was truly excited to be there with me. The bad feelings didn't seem to take him over until a few days later. One would think it would hit him the next morning, but these morning times were lovely. August would spend some time shaving and washing his face, while I would stand at the bathroom door and watch him. I loved to see him there naked in front of the big mirror. He was not disturbed by my presence in the doorway—he had never been modest—and although our intimate times were few and far between, he had never denied me this.

I would make a pot of coffee for us both, and he would fix some bagels and peanut butter. Nothing was ever said about our time the evening before. He always smiled at me in the morning. He hardly, if ever, smiled otherwise. It was such a shock to hear him to say what he did in that phone call. It was just more evidence of his dual personalities, the twins that were threatening my hard-won balance and precarious stability.

# Self-Rising Flower

Up until then, I thought that if I prayed enough, the lord would deliver August to me, deliver his dark body, dark hair, and the square head I so enjoyed holding.

Who was I kidding? I no more believed in the lord than I did Santa Claus. My friend JR said that I was just pretending to love him, and that this was impossible because I should know that two men can't really be together. JR is in his eighties and comes from a completely different generation, a generation that felt that gay people were the scum of the earth and somehow not worthy of being taken seriously. The word he used most often was *fairy*. I turned this word around and said to myself yes, fairies have wings, and didn't I have wings when I survived my first encounter with schizophrenia? Didn't I rise above it and use it to my advantage? My first night in the hospital those years ago started with my intake. There was a strapping kind of redneck guy who did this information taking. He had referred to me immediately as his buttercup. He knew who I was, knew my family and my background. It was a small town and most of the people were familiar with us farm kids. They knew the stories of our famous play house, of us entertaining the farm workers with our singing and dancing. They knew of my grandmother's award-winning roses and her membership in that ancient congregation, and they also knew about us collecting the daffodil flowers and bringing them to the hospital for the poor. I was surprised that this man was taking so much care with me. Now, I try to picture his face, but I can only remember him calling me his buttercup and the big work boots he wore under his scrubs.

In the beginning, all of the nurses thought I was taking drugs. When they asked me if this was true, I initially said yes. I thought they were talking about the cold medicine I had bought a day or so earlier. I also thought it might be the thyme I had received on a trip to the Bahamas. I had gone on an adventure in Nassau where I searched for my collegemate's mother in a very poor and dangerous area of the island. After several tries, I had caught a jitney bus out to Blue Hill Road and located my friend's fruit stand. Before I left from my visit, the Bahamians had loaded me up with dried conch and a bagful of the herb thyme. They told me it would cure anything, so when I returned to the states, I rolled it and smoked some. This was just a few days before I was hospitalized; the association had not been that far off. Little did I know that the chemicals in my brain were draining out faster than a beaver pond with a broken dam. It was nothing I had done to myself, nothing I had taken or smoked, just an inherited brain disorder from my crazy uncle Johnny, the uncle who had chased my cousin through the fields with a homemade hatchet, and the uncle I had found dead in the bed I slept in when I was a young boy.

I spent three days in the psyche ward of my small-town hospital. I was cared for by a female doctor named Gwen. She was a large woman with a red afro and huge bug sunglasses. She suffered from Multiple Sclerosis, and was very sympathetic to me since she was ill herself. I felt as though I were a damaged person, but I managed to get myself together, like Lazarus rising from the grave, still wobbly and paranoid, and was released. From then on, I marked that point as when my life truly began. After that, I could hardly remember ever being free of schizophrenia.

# A Slice of the Watermelon Moon

I doubt very seriously that August would have sympathized with my state of mind. In fact, I doubted he would sympathize with anyone. He didn't seem to have compassion for any being whatsoever. Speaking with his classy ex-girlfriend one day on the phone, she let this slip: he would let you borrow any amount of money or feed any stranger, but as far as real compassion, he had none. Telling a sad story to him was like talking to a stone: his face would freeze up, and his comments were often so harsh as to create a chill up one's spine. All the time, he thought he was acting in the most prudent manner. He was much like Agnes in this sense and felt he was more than fair. He always mistook horror and pain for mere storytelling. If he had the chance, I am sure he would have made me a story too. Of course, he would leave out the intimate parts, but we would be just a bit of mountain lore or, if I was lucky, a tale to tell to some gay trucker under the neon sign of a roadside diner. Still, he was the effervescent, masculine comet that had flown through my radar, and I loved him dearly.

# City Slick Stranger

Although I was born in the country, and raised on our farm, this is not readily apparent...or at least, I hope not. Most true Southerners have a little bit of a chip on their shoulders where this is concerned. Southern people have been so stereotyped and stigmatized that it almost becomes a social paranoia, especially when they are travelling the United States. Also, this paranoia is present within the boundaries of Dixie itself. There are so many different types of accents and ways of being in Georgia alone that you almost have to be an expert to navigate it. I have always thought I was pretty good at this, but occasionally I have found myself if not in danger, at least in a kind of communication hurricane. When physical violence is threatening, the Southern preacher comes out, or in some cases, the witch doctor or oracle. The poor people of this great state, usually due to money or perceived class, have a very large chip on their shoulder, and they don't like to mix with others. My times with August were always constantly throwing me into a cauldron of the most interesting hot pepper brew, and I had to be perennially on my toes. This was quadrupled because not only am I a city slicker, but I am also a homosexual.

Oftentimes I did not come out a winner. Sometimes I miscalculated and was barely tolerated by August's friends, as was the case with Ed. Ed was a truck driver for August's old company. He had a very handsome but wrinkled face, and he was married to a pretty but toothless, small woman named Towanna. They had a young son, who one night during a party saved my life—I ended up with a large, nasty scar on my forehead to prove it. Ed Junior always had a sack of pot on him, and this is what led to my doomed attempt to impress the locals, and scattered August's pretense to the north, south, east, west and, the most damaging, a bunch of old men with whom he use to work.

"It was a verbal ambush," I said to Possum.

I wasn't even sure Possum would know what verbal ambush meant, but that is what is was—a complete bamboozle!

"He just came right out and asked me! He just came right out and said it!" I screamed.

I was still high and drunk, and I'm sure pathetic at that stage.

"I'm like the eight-track gorilla at the six, six, six house in Athens! My mind goes in ten different directions when I'm stoned!"

I was still yelling and starting to feel physically ill.

"What in the hell are you talking about?" Possum asked.

"I don't care, I simply don't care. I live in Athens, they live in bum-fuck nowhere!"

I was deluding myself. "We were under the barn cover and I thought he was asking about you!" I mumbled.

"What are you talking about? Tell me!" Possum said.

"Ed asked me if 'he' was gay. I thought he was asking about you, and I nodded my head and said yes! He was actually asking about August, I think, and I said yes! I didn't know what he meant until we left in your pickup truck! If August finds out about what I said, he's going to knock my teeth out!"

My brain froze then and my hand tick started, where I rub my fingers together so fast it causes a cramp, my arm moves too, and the worry sets in.

"I plan on clearing this little mess up with Ed," I said. "He likes me, and he loves August a whole bunch. I think he'll be receptive."

It wasn't like I thought of being thought of as gay as a bad thing, but I knew August wasn't quite like me, and I didn't want anything to shine a negative light on him, especially when it wasn't true. He had always let it be known that he didn't want people to gossip about him. The old trucker men had heard mine and Ed's little exchange. They were standing around the low country boil pot while Ed and I smoked. I wondered what they would say.

# Question

I asked my friend Leigh, what it meant that he would not even turn over and face me when we were in the bed, but if I placed my arm around his chest, my hand between his breasts, he would not let go. I asked her this question and, more frequently, asked myself. I wondered if August had begun to think of his mortality upon this clutching— could it be that he really did not want to let me go? I had thought about losing him a lot since he was so much older than myself, and even imagined the funeral, Agnes and his daughter sitting on one side of the church and me wailing away on the other side. I did not think I could handle it; it was a very morbid thought I'd admit, but it did cross my mind.

I was lying with August in the bed, under his heavy quilts, one night and had a question.

"Do you know what I am to you?" I asked.

He answered with a humored, "What?"

"Do you know? Do you really know?"

"Can you think for a minute in the old South way of seeing things?" He was confused and rolled over to look at me.

"I'll tell you if you want to know." I was being a little mysterious. "I'm your bedfellow!"

"What do you mean?" He was completely at a loss, as was usually the case when I became the rebel.

"I am your bedfellow! Every man worth his snuff has or has had a bedfellow!"

"Cecil, I don't have a clue what the hell you're talking about!" He snorted.

"I am the one who, after all your women friends have given up on you, and called you a son of a bitch, and taken all your money, and made you feel guilty, I am the one who will be here to love you and rub your sore neck in this here bed, until one of us no longer can. That is what they call a bedfellow!" I stated.

"When I was a kid, there was a neighboring farm where three brothers lived: Sid, Francis, and Ferral French. They had about two thousand acres and lived in a huge white house with columns and screened-in porches, the whole typical Southern shebang," I said.

"My daddy and I used to go over there for Christmas, and they would fix dozens of fruit cakes covered in cheese cloth and soaked in rum. They would let me pick out some small piece of antique furniture from their ancient attic and take it home to my mother. You can imagine how thrilled I was!

"Not one of these brothers had ever been married, but Sid and Francis lived in the mansion together, and Ferral lived in a small, white, double front door cottage across the sandy dirt road. Sid was the more feminine brother, Francis always seemed stiff and masculine, and Ferral, being the only one who lived alone, was the more passionate and independent. We were related to these brothers in some obtuse way, and my father always held them in high regard, as did I. Although these interesting and lovely men were brothers, I am quite sure they were bedfellows, kinda like you and me.

"Unfortunately, a tragedy happened when I was a little older. Ferral, being the independent person that he was, took an outside lover. My daddy always called him a fishing buddy, but it was a lover nonetheless. Anyway, he took a lover, but one day Ferral's lover did not show up for supper, and was later discovered shot dead in the woods, an obvious hunting accident, or so it was said. For several weeks, Ferral did not leave his cottage, and two months later, he took his life with a thirty-eight pistol to the heart. One year later exactly to the date, Mr. Sid took his life, and Francis followed later."

I was holding back tears when I told August this story that night. He grabbed me by the balls, digging in with his fingernails, and said nothing. I reached over his left shoulder and put my hand on his breast, slowly peeled his white briefs from his body, and snuggled up close to him. I could feel his heart beating and the sun-tanned warmth covering his back and legs. He pressed his ass to me, and after a while, I heard light slobbery breathing and his fitful sleep murmurs.

# Electric Light Barn Party

The Choctaw bull dozier was standing in the center of August's barn, poised to throw his shiny dart at the bulls-eye of the black and red board. Girdy had just hopped through the side door of the barn, boyfriend in tow, and Possum, August, and I were peering into the freezer, looking for some frozen sausages and the bottle of Blue Ice vodka Bull had purchased. It was my birthday, and August had graciously agreed to host the party.

August was wearing his tight jeans and cowboy boots, Bull was wearing a pair of track pants and t-shirt, since he was so big he could hardly get anything else to fit, I had dressed up for August in my own country boy attire, and the only accessories Possum had were his little dog Elvis and an English driving cap. Girdy's boyfriend had walked in the door with a nasty scratch on his face, which August told me Girdy had caused. Girdy was looking kind of haggard since she had been in the hospital for a few days. She was tired, but her mouth was loud as ever.

At the party were Girdy's boyfriend, a Florida scuba diver slash bridge inspector; Girdy, the flatfooted redneck woman; Bull, the oversized Puerto Rican loving bad boy; Possum and his Chihuahua, called the Pelvis since they could not be separated; me, the urban gay man; and August, the owner and operator of the electric light honky-tonk barn.

August shut the lid of his freezer. We had just recovered the sausages and booze. He sat down next to Bull and stared at me.

"Cecil, what the hell is wrong with you?" he asked. "You look like Gayle's uncle over there; you haven't said a word. What's on your mind?"

I perked up and looked at him. "Actually there's nothing on my mind for a change. That's probably what you're seeing."

He was referring to the German man who had been so strange, and whose family had experienced so much strife, even suicide. I kind of liked this association; Gayle's uncle had been a smart and eccentric man. Exactly the kind of person he and Girdy might talk about.

August told me a story about him one day. He said that Gayle's uncle once put an ad in the newspaper seeking an employee for his textile mill. A young black woman had responded to the ad and come to his house. The first thing the German man said was that not only was the woman to perform her company duties, but she was also required to suck his dick whenever he wanted. To say the least, this did not go over very well with the woman's family, and later that evening, they showed up to defend their family honor. He, of course, had been through this before and leveled a shotgun out the door. He said that was part of the job and that was that. I knew all of this and thought it was amusing.

August and I had had sex for two nights in a row before the party, and it had given me warm feelings towards him. We also had a kind of secret language to be used in front of Bull and others. Our secret language consisted of this: if August wanted me to spend the night and we had company over, he was to wear the hat I bought him at Yosemite National Park in California or the T-shirt I bought him in Waikiki—the one that said *north shore*. If he just wanted a little attention around back, he was to wear the pink T-shirt I brought him from San Francisco. Sounds crazy, but the code worked quite well and was always exciting, since I never knew what he would be wearing. Sometimes he would trick me and just wear black. He knew I couldn't resist him in black, and come hell or high water, I was going to be next to him.

It being my birthday that night, he wore the hat and the north shore T-shirt at the same time!

August had a potbelly stove situated in the corner of his barn. That night, Bull put a can of boiled peanuts on the eye of the stove, a warm Southern delight, and also buttered and salted potatoes on the hot fire. We had our usual fierce game of darts and ate the entire container of peanuts. The main attraction was the trucker steaks August prepared on the grill, and the mess of turnip greens he mixed with hot pepper sauce from our farm. He did not have a large cooking repertoire, since he had eaten out all those years on the road, but his marinated steaks were always a big hit with the crowd.

August's ability to entertain was endless, and he had been entertaining Bull for over three weeks as they built an addition on his barn. He was one of the most generous people I ever had the great pleasure of knowing and just about the only thing I wanted for my birthday. That, of course, happened, and the night sailed on into the cool January morning.

# Sweet and Sour Possum

Possum is my third cousin; of this, we can be certain. We had learned this little bit of information by accident, but it is true nonetheless. I called him Possum because he had menacing teeth and a large nose. His more striking features were offset by his bald head, and soft eyes. He also liked to catch the little marsupials with his Have-a-Heart-Trap and release them into the neighboring wealthy subdivision. He got a kick out of doing this because he thought the subdivision people were completely crazy, and also intruders from the now-declining old town of Macon, Georgia.

I have mentioned before that coincidences are angles that co-incide, and this was true of Possum, because he lived around the way from August. Can you imagine that I met August on the interstate under illegal circumstances in Florida, and he brings me right back to my dear Possum? I don't believe in a god with a personality, but you could say he or she has a sense of humor!

Possum doesn't hear very well, and subsequently uses a loud voice. He is also not a very good communicator, so when we do have a conversation, it warms my heart and makes me feel close to him. We have been together for over ten years, and had many good times on vacation trips and camping at the nude campground. He loves to be naked, and has a nice stout body covered in blonde hair from head to toe. His little dog Elvis is the joy of his life, and brings us together like parents. Possum

67

has a talent for math and can do any formula in his head. His grammar is atrocious though, and he sounds like a country boy from the depths of the swamp. He loves to collect art, and has a collection that is worth more than the grey shack in which he lives. He seemed  when we met to be the perfect combination of a gay man stuck in a straight body, not a bisexual like August, but a country man that had not lived under the unfortunate influence of the queeny and masked gay people in larger cities. The word Botox never entered into his vocabulary, but he did try Rogaine for his bald head—it just caused a burning rash.

Possum has a good sense of humor, but it is often veiled in a "they did me wrong" kind of attitude. He owns a whole series of books that suggests ways to sabotage people, and because of this, he thinks he's been red-flagged by the FBI or CIA. If a plane or helicopter flies by, he is certain they are on a surveillance mission, scoping out his green house or nonexistent liquor still. He's quite a hoarder, and the green house is full of electrical supplies and buckets of dirt, not marijuana, and the nonexistent still is a large stainless steel cauldron filled with aluminum cans.

Possum is a collector, a baker of cakes, an experienced electrician, a church member, and has saved me many times with his masculine presence and no-nonsense attitude. He is also a reader of books and, contrary to his country voice and attitude, a very smart and one could say modern man. He claims to be a pagan, and in a sense, it is true, but I have the sneaking suspicion he secretly prays to Jesus every now and then. He would deny this, but he is a Southerner that grew up in a small, rural Baptist church, and I think this kind of upbringing never truly leaves the mind, unless it is expelled in the most dramatic and alarming psychological fashion.

The only things that are alarming about dear Possum are his loud voice and a seething, almost hidden, temper. He has never hit or really yelled at me, but I sometimes feel as though it is a real possibility. I think his anger comes out at his workplace. He's in the construction industry and is surrounded by a bunch of immature and reckless kids, a redneck, idiot foreman, and a sickening, Southern Baptist boss. He's not afraid to be out at his job, and this sometimes scares me. One little "accident" and he would no longer be with me. So far, nothing that dramatic or terrible has happened, just a few mean-spirited words and looks, but the threat of it has me worried.

# Cabin Fever

"You're gonna have to go home tonight," August slurred.

We had just finished playing a game of darts, and I knew August was scheduled to go on a riding trip the next morning. I suspected he didn't want my car to be seen in his driveway, or for me to be there when the gang arrived. The "gang" was a sixty-nine-year-old county worker with curly white hair and a filthy mouth, and his sweet wife, who had a bad denture job and could hear less than nothing. Sometimes they would come over on the weekends, and I guess they wondered why I was always present. August did not have the foresight to tell them I was his best friend and always blamed me for what people might think. I guess it was just the age difference. I mentioned that, in my neck of the woods, it wasn't unusual for friends to be together more often, and not just on the weekends.

Possum and Girdy were there too. We had just cooked a delicious steak and the super-hot Cajun sausage Possum brought over. Girdy and dear Possum were not part of the dart game. They would just mill around while August and I got competitive. Girdy was drinking her Coors Light and Possum always had some sort of dark foreign brew. He could only drink a few before he was intoxicated, and Girdy always had to leave early to be with her ailing husband. I was becoming tipsy too, and announced that I would be leaving with Girdy.

Out of nowhere, August jumped to my side and whispered,

"Stay with me tonight." This was a complete turnaround from the beginning of the evening, and a late surprise to the ending of the game.

I walked over to the potbelly stove and grabbed a handful of boiled peanuts; they had been steeping all night and were nice and hot. I filled my plastic cup with ice and poured myself another vodka tonic, then sat down in the camouflage camping chair. I was waiting for some kind of explanation as to why August had changed his mind. This kind of reversal was practically unheard of in our history; I was so used to disappointments that I truly wondered what he was thinking. August motioned for me to lean over the canvas chair.

"I knew you didn't want to leave," he whispered.

I nodded my head to show that I understood, and that I would stay. He always had the knack for making my heart beat just a little bit faster and adding that extra dimension to my life.

"I didn't want to leave you blue," he said.

It was always funny when he used *that* language where I might use something romantic or intellectual. It was very effective, and he knew it. Girdy took her exit, as did Possum, and we were left alone.

"You want to have another game of darts or you want to go to bed?" August asked.

I grabbed his square head and ran my fingers through his crew cut.

"I'm ready to go to bed, you scalawag, what do you think?"

I was imagining his high bed and his grandmother's handmade quilt, all exactly right for his room in the cabin and, of course, his hot, almond-scented body pressed next to me.

"I've got something for you," August murmured.

"What is it? I asked.

"Just something I want you to have."

He unzipped the front of my black leather jacket, and slowly, as if holding something precious, slipped a thick gold chain into my pocket. There was something dangling from the end of it, but right then, I couldn't tell what it was.

"My mother gave me this when I was a little boy, but I want you to have it."

We closed off the side doors to the barn and shut the lid on the stove. It was very dark outside so I held onto his shirt and followed him through the red mud to the front door of the cabin. My shoes were covered in muck, so I took them off, and also decided to remove my jeans and shirt. There was always some little argument as to where I would sleep. I usually said I would rest on the sofa, but we both knew I would be naked and under his covers before he even had time to clean his teeth. I jumped up on the bed and poked my head up from the pillows, watching him closely. He was sixty years old, but his ass and legs were those of someone decades younger. He looked like a stripper I had seen one time, and I loved him for this! He had the habit of walking on his toes when he was naked. This made him look like a gazelle, elegant and light and peaceful, like he might just sneak up on me and tell a joke.

August was apt to do this—tell me a joke I mean. He had the most peculiar sense of humor. Agnes had been so nasty to him through the years that I think it had developed rather slowly and, almost like a good bottle of wine, had become very sophisticated. He could point out your faults and at the same time make you laugh at yourself and at him too. All the while, he was very serious. This made him a star, always, and that was exactly what was dangling from the end of the gold chain he gave me: a tiny, shiny, gold Star of David, his mother's gift to him, and now a special gift to me. Later, I would take the star off the chain and place it on my forearm. The hot Southern sun would tan the outline of the memory into my skin, a temporary, close reminder of this beautiful man that only the pale, cool light of the watermelon moon could remove.

# The Hen and the Rooster

August and I were sitting on his back deck one late afternoon when he slowly told me that he had been hired by a new trucking company and that he was going to go back on the road. I wouldn't see him for months on end. I left that day without having even one drink and felt like a slug. I went back to dear Possum's house and took a sedative to relax. We had a nice night, but I was visibly disturbed. The next day, I drove back to Athens, Georgia, and got drunk. I called August early that evening and told him this story on the phone.

"I'm mad as an old, wet Southern hen at you!" I said.

"What do you mean, and why?" he asked.

"Well, one time there was this old, wet, Southern hen, and Lord have mercy, she loved this old, red, Northern rooster! The old, red, Northern rooster wasn't aware that that old wet, Southern hen loved him, so he always stayed detached and thought about other chickens. One day in passing, that old, red, Northern rooster told the old, wet, Southern hen that he was about to go on a journey, a long journey. He told that old, wet, Southern hen that he would be going to the state of Chickasaw—you know, the one with the Ozark mountains—and that he would be traveling to Chickallas, and then even as far north as New Chick City, up near the Hudson River. 'Your life is going to change!' said the old red, Northern rooster. Well, the old, wet, Southern hen knew what this meant, and Lord have mercy, she

75

didn't want her life to change that much. And Lord have mercy, if she could do anything about it, it wouldn't."

I told August this stupid little story in the hopes that he would reconsider going back to work. If only he would just budget his money, I argued, he wouldn't have to. I had several different motivations for this, the main one being that I wouldn't see him for months. I guess I was being selfish, and he probably knew what he needed, but I was concerned. I always kind of worried about his safety when he was on the road; one time, I was even convinced I saw his truck on television. They were showing a horrible wreck on the Bay Bridge in San Francisco and I panicked. The truck was cantilevered off the bridge, just waiting to fall into the icy water. I think I saw stars and heard "Ave Maria". It was probably that little angel on my shoulder telling my mind, "Yeah, look, there's your guy hanging over the bridge, we've got you now." Luckily, I called and he answered his cell phone; it wasn't him. He was sitting at the In-N-Out Burger on the Embarcadero having lunch.

# Return to the Road

August was set to return to the road, but this time, it would be a little different. He would have to stay the nights in the truck, and none of his expenses would be paid. He was not too upset about this, but I wondered if he would be happy with this new trucking company. He was going to make a trip to West Virginia to retrieve his birth certificate from the courthouse because the new company needed his records and also to visit his cousin Buddy. For many years, I had heard stories of Buddy. He lived on the West Virginia border, and was quite a character I was told. Supposedly, he sold T-shirts and trinkets to every gas station and truck stop from South Carolina up to Pennsylvania and had amassed a huge fortune. Buddy lived in an old, run-down apartment building, even though he could afford a nice house, and he gave copious amounts of money to the local public high school. According to August, he'd had not a few male lovers during his lifetime and liked to go to the town's lively dinner theater. As far as I was concerned, the apple did not fall far from the old tree.

A few days before August was to go on the road, we had a fish fry, a delectable Southern tradition. I spent several hours helping him clean the cabin and get the yard ready for the party. This was to be his last hurrah before he returned to work. Every night I spent with him before the party, he went directly to his bedroom and shut the paneled door. I was left alone on the floor—no intimacy whatsoever. A depression set in over me, and during the lively party, I just sat on the porch with hardly any energy and barely anything to say to the guests. This bit of festivity in the woods was mounting up to be, in my head, a requiem instead of a celebration. August, of course, took no notice of my disturbance and entertained the troops like a professional.

The days were not all bad though. He had been in the sun, was turning a nice shade of brown, and was also growing his hair out. This created a nice tension in my crazy head, the kind of tension between what you really want and what you cannot possibly have. I knew at the very least this would lead to a burst of creative energy. I only had to wait for it to happen, grab hold of me, twist my attention, and throw me into a world, not of loneliness, but rather forward movement. In my own small way, I thanked my dear August for this opportunity.

The morning after the fish fry, the sun crept through the windows and illuminated the cabin walls and Ed's white tube socks, still wrapped around his feet and sticking off the recliner. I crawled from my stack of quilts on the floor and zigzagged my way to the kitchen counter. Ed didn't stir, but I could hear August cleaning his false teeth in the bathroom and humming the tune he had been thinking of the whole weekend. It was a happy little hum, and the morning was peaceful. I was glad he was up early, and I was expecting him to meet me on the front porch for coffee.

August loved good South American coffee so I quickly brewed a pot of the strong elixir, rubbed Ed's funny, bald head to see if he wanted a cup—he didn't—and walked out to the front porch. He has a fabulous, wide porch that runs from one side of the cabin to the other. It's actually facing away from the road, but August always insisted on calling it the front porch, not the back. Properly, it's a veranda with antique lantern lights hanging on either side and a western, ghost-town facade center-stage for him to conduct business and pleasure against.

August finally padded his way onto the porch, and asked if we had any coffee. I stared at him for a moment. The only thing he had on was a pair of tighty-whities. He had been drying everything on a clothesline and they were stretched and droopy. It was a funny, but sexy, sight. The drawers hung off his hips and gave me a peek at his tan line. He wasn't aware of his appeal, so he walked past me and took a leak off the side rail. There is an old saying in the South that states if a man can't pee off his own front porch, he doesn't want to live there. It came natural to all the guys that would visit the cabin, but sometimes I wondered if one or two curious trespassers had caught a glimpse of us in full glory, maybe getting some kind of erotic, rural thrill.

I had been caught in the buff at Spider Hill several times; more often than not, it was the young game warden snooping around my mother's old concrete pool. He was a harmless fellow that I imagined never got what he wanted from his girlfriend or wife and so decided to take a risk and spy on me. My thoughts weren't all paranoia, and August's house occasionally became a theater for my own personal enjoyment.

August finally plopped down into the wooden rocking chair, tan and all, and lit a cigarette. I leaned up and asked him if he had one for me. He took the pack out of the chair's cup holder and handed it over.

"The trucking company said that they do allow the drivers to take another person on the road, but you know we have to sleep in the cab," he said.

I had asked him about this a few weeks before, but I didn't expect the answer to be yes. The sun was suddenly shining brighter, and I became a little excited. My first thought happened to be, *He wants me to go.* My second was, *Where are we going to sleep? In some rest area or truck stop?*

My head snapped toward him and I piped up. "What about the lot lizards?" Agnes had used this phrase to refer to the sucky-sucky boys and prostitutes she imagined August to be friends with. "Won't we be surrounded by thieves and hitchhikers and axe murderers, and all sorts of unsavory characters?"

"Cecil, this is not the nineteen seventies. There are cameras everywhere at these pit stops, and for that matter, how do you think we met? You were flashing me on the highway!" He laughed.

This was totally true, but I never thought I was being trashy, just an exhibitionist, an artist, if you will, a horny college guy! My psychiatrist told me it was nothing more serious than a teen-ager mooning someone as he drove to Panama City for spring break. The priest that I consulted did not take it so lightly and suggested I repent and see a better therapist, preferably a member of the church—maybe even a nun!

"I got ya," I said.

"When can we go?"

"Let me get acclimated to the new company rules and then we'll see," he said.

# Thirty-Eight Special

Ed's next fish fry was delicious, all fried up and golden brown. August and I were entertaining the rednecks and Possum was paying us a visit. We were all celebrating August turning down the third job, and Bull's marriage to his Puerto Rican bride. The one thing we had not counted on was Girdy's Floridian boyfriend's jealousy toward August. It manifested in such a dramatic way that we were all left in a little bit of a daze, not to mention the heavy smell of gunpowder and lead.

The party started all well and good. One would think that after eating eight pounds of fish fried in Crisco and dozens of hushpuppies, the mood would be sedate.

This was usually the case when handsome Ed was at the helm of the outdoor deep fryer and everyone was feeling the sun and humidity and lard running through their bloodstream, but Girdy's camper-dwelling boyfriend had other ideas.

We knew there was going to be trouble when Girdy's boyfriend wandered up to the barn with a bloated red face and slurred speech. The Grayberry newspaper had stated that a week prior he had approached poor old Girdy and her husband's doublewide with a rifle and demanded a beer. That had ended with the husband firing his shotgun through the trailer door and four Grayberry police officers confiscating the weapons and hauling the boyfriend off to jail.

I wondered to myself if the rumors were true that he had

a ten-inch cock and that Girdy had such a hot piece of ass he just couldn't let it go and go back to Tampa to his overweight wife and son. August was approaching him at that moment and telling him to do just that. Get the hell off his property, and go back home!

Boyfriend was having none of it though. Home is where the heart is, and I guess his heart was with Girdy and his nineteen seventy-six RV truck parked in her backyard. The thing he was not counting on in that moment of passion was August's thirty eight special, tucked into his cargo shorts pocket, and a very crazy and agitated tank-top-wearing guest's willingness to blow his head clean off his beach bum shoulders.

After a couple of dry runs, the boyfriend had decided it would be in his best interest to follow August's instructions and leave the compound. He made it about three hundred feet past the gate and stopped on the dirt road, right in front of the old barn. The tank-top wearer was kind of milling around with the shotgun on his shoulder. He had his hairy chest poked out, crucifix and all, and was threatening to shoot. I told him he better not—I was trying to be diplomatic, and he certainly didn't want to end up in prison for killing an idiot.

Possum walked away towards the washhouse, to get out of range, and the women seemed not to know what to do. Tank-top's girlfriend was so full of pain pills that she had lost all fear and was just hanging around waiting for the next vodka tonic and her favorite song on the radio. All the while, I noticed August fiddling with his little snub-nosed gun in his pocket. This all happened in about three quick minutes, but it felt like forever.

When August fired his first shots, it took me by surprise. I had not expected him to actually do it, but he took aim above the boyfriend's truck and let loose! I think it scared him a little, and he regretted it later, but Florida boy got the message and tore off down the road. Everyone calmed down, the pork butt was removed from the grill, more drinks were poured, and Girdy said her apologies, as any true Southern woman would.

# Muff Divers, Oil Riggers, and a Little Bit of Hot Sauce

I wondered if August knew that his married neighbor and masculine oil rigger friend had decided that I should come around and have a little fun with him—sexually, I mean. The sex part was tempting, but I was in no way going to partake in his crank habit. We had already witnessed one of August's hunter buddies go down in flames because of a slight crack addiction, and I was just not willing to follow him to the yearlong rehab clinic, giving up booze, cigarettes, and my lovely weekends with my Jewish lover.

The attraction began innocently enough. Bull declared, in a drunken conversation, that he was the world's number one muff diver of all time, and that his now wife was a pecan tan Puerto Rican, her beauty the likes of which none had ever seen. Bull did not have a conventional sense of humor, nor did he have a wicked sense of humor, but he was known to make broad, sweeping statements that were oftentimes quite true and always funny. This was one of those statements, and that's when the revelation happened. As revelations go, this one was a little shocking, but nothing I had not come to expect at August's cabin.

"Ok, Bull, if you're a muff diver, what am I?" I asked.

I was standing in the big barn doorway, a little tipsy, and Bull was giving me a big hug, as he always did, his large bovine eyes kinda rolling around in his square head. Stepping back, he patiently looked me over and said, "I don't really have an answer for that."

Well, this had been the opening the sexy oil rigger had been looking for, and he flew over to my side and blurted out that I was the "big pipeline surveyor," and always welcome on his excursions to the gulf coast, and indeed would probably be welcomed by his other comrades.

At that moment, one of his friendly oil worker buddies was in August's barn, listening to our conversation. I looked over to see him jumping around, pulling his shirt up, and practically doing a private strip tease for me. I asked the buddy to come nearer to me. I could not recall ever feeling skin so soft, it was like butter. I ran my hands all over his muscular chest, all the way up to his hard nipples. They weren't pierced like mine are and he shuddered a bit. I shuddered too but couldn't keep my eyes off the first oil rigger's hairy belly. He too was pulling his shirt up and giving me a grand view. Had my miserable luck changed, or was I just being led into temptation by this married man and his young, young buddy?

Later that night, as I was trying to go to sleep, I uttered the Lord's Prayer a couple of times, always emphasizing the "lead us not into temptation" part. I also secretly got up while August was sleeping and dumped a half bottle of hot sauce into the roast he was cooking. I thought it might spice him up a little. As if things weren't hot enough.

# Fire Wood and Fire Water

August Kammer insisted that the piece of gnarled pinewood looked like an octopus. He had dragged it down from the old barn and was going to put it on the embers that were burning from the night before. One of our private and soft pastimes was staring into the fire ring and imagining what animal or object we could see emerging from the coals. I was always captivated by what August could interpret. He kept his imagination hidden from other people, so I was surprised every time he let it run wild when I was present.

He carefully built the fire as the sun went down and a pink glow was cast on the surrounding trees and the rocks that encircled the wood. I went into the cabin while he was working and poured us a glassful of the moonshine he had bought from a man down the road. I mixed it with a little hard apple cider and a few cubes of ice then sat down by the fire. August was fiddling with his cell phone, but he noticed that I wasn't saying very much. I was trying hard to look into the fire and see an animal or something, but my mind was on the statement he had made earlier in the evening. I guess I was not in as festive a mood as he was. He had mentioned, in a passing moment, that he was not in the mood for any kind of sexual activity, and really never was. He said that if he was a "truly gay" person, he would give me a little more attention than he did, but I should know that that never happened.

It had actually happened plenty enough, but I knew what he was saying. I always called him my reluctant lover, and it was true in a way. I think I misinterpreted his actions under the quilt as intoxication rather than shear rejection. His guilt was rather odd. It seemed to overtake him right at the point where he might step over the precipice and accept me, but instead he let it take over and control him. I had seen this happen a few times with some of the men I had been interested in over the years. They would reveal their soft side to me, I would open myself to them, but the next thing I knew, these men would run away into the arms of the wrong woman, shut me out, and then a baby would be on the way. Divorce usually followed, along with withering looks directed at me from the guilty and angry father. It was as if I was a cupid, but my arrows hit the guys in the ass instead of the heart.

# *Christmas*

Naked and snuggled under the quilts, I waited for August to finish his beer and cigarette. The day had been one of me cleaning the cabin, and a night of drinking vodka tonics and eating tortilla dip with processed cheese. It was freezing outside and the windows were steamed up from the gas heater August had in his great room. It always took him a good while to wind down from the evening, so I decided to just climb under the covers and feel the cotton quilts on my body. My great grandmother owned quilts like this when she was alive and there is nothing more comforting than one of these patchwork animals draped heavily over you.

Mr. Kammer's quilts smelled like wheat straw, just like his crew cut, and they had to be at least a hundred years old, although I felt like I was eighteen! It was Christmas, after all, and I was ready to have August next to me. He usually turned off his cell phone and closed the farm gate, but that particular night, we had neglected to do this. That's when the phone rang.

Sometimes, since I have a mental illness, in particular schizophrenia, I can't always interpret what is being said in other rooms or far away from me. If what is going on is one thing, I might hear it as another. In any case, I thought it was Bull on the phone asking if he could come over. I thought he had had an argument or something with his wife and needed a place to crash. I hadn't had a psychotic episode in over a decade, but what I was hearing was either my mistake or a wrong number—so I thought. Then I heard August speaking in a really sweet tone, with a voice he almost never used when talking to me, and I realized he was on the phone with a woman. It wasn't just any woman either, it was the truly psychotic and herpetic Maria, with bleach blonde hair and gigantic boobs! She was asking August if it would be okay for her to spend the night at the cabin.

Layer by layer, I removed the quilts, touched the cold pine floor with my feet and got up. August was still on the phone with the woman, but I knew there wouldn't be any intimacy that night. If I could have crawled through the phone lines, I would have, strangling her and disposing of the body in an efficient manner. I knew that August never took our lovemaking seriously. It was, again, the take me or leave me attitude, but I certainly thought that just maybe I was a little bit more tempting than some psychotic Mexican woman with a herpes breakout!

# Discovery

After the herpes scare, I was left with a kind of bitter feeling towards August Kammer. Nothing had really changed except I was stuck, every morning, checking my cock for any signs of the disease. He assured me that he didn't "tap that ass" and nothing would ever happen, but I was not so confident. Agnes had made sure I would always be wary of whatever came out of his mouth, and I knew that he basically always fed his associates at least a line or two. I'm not saying he was dishonest, but he loved to calm the waters, and give people what they considered the best possible idea of themselves. I have always been a lucid dreamer, and this holiday time had made that go into overdrive. January was coming up, and it was always tough for me. Psychotic episodes had occurred during the winter before, and this ripple in my brain was just the thing needed to set me off.

Contrary to my paranoid brain's opinion, spring came and everything was ok down below and with August. The Florida sunshine had seeped across the border into Georgia and the dogwoods and buttercups bloomed as usual. My hidden monster of a mental illness had only grabbed me for an instant instead of tearing me down into terrifying shreds. I was more than thankful for this, and August didn't even seem to notice. He was truly not aware of the acid that ran through my temporal lobes and had, at times, even denied the fact that I could suddenly become very ill. He had not witnessed my disintegration as Possum had.

Possum had seen me go from a relatively carefree, happy person to a scared and sick man curled up on his brown Baker sofa, paralyzed by fear. I give dear Possum the credit for keeping me stable, although it wasn't anything that he did per se. He just didn't leave me. He would let me go through the episode without exacerbating it. He didn't have a terrific amount of patience with me during a breakdown, but at least he didn't throw me out, and he would always tell me what was true. It was in his nature to be honest. It was also in his nature to be brutally honest, and that's what he did one month later.

Possum and I had not had sex in over five years and he was getting quite jealous of my relationship with August. The word came in that Possum was fucking tired of me coming down to visit and that he didn't want me anymore. I wasn't surprised that he had lost interest. I had lost interest too, but it wasn't because of my attraction to August. Nobody had ever done it better than August, but Possum had always been my first love, and I would be grateful for the rest of my life for his simple kindness and direction. I took his abrupt exit from my life as almost a kind of relief.

I discovered it was more for him than for me. He had his small rural radius, and I had August, the worldly Jewish trucker from West Virginia. My temporal existence had been enhanced by both personalities!

# *High Octane*

The devastating moonshine explosion was equivalent to the immense detonation I felt in my chest, namely the area of my heart. August had picked up the can of high-octane liquid without me noticing and poured it onto the hot coals. The flames reached out and licked Bull, setting him on fire immediately! His entire sweater was engulfed with the volatile stuff, and it crawled up his arms and legs.

I had bought us two steaks earlier that evening, before Bull arrived and was expecting for August and I to have them later after he departed. I was also half way expecting us to be intimate in the late hours. Bull left early to tend his burns and August and I had a nice roll in his pillow top bed. I got up during the night to smoke a cigarette on the porch, and he joined me and the dog on this wooden veranda. The moon was beaming down through the sheets and clothes he had hanging outside from the ceiling, and I could vaguely hear the sounds of a bass guitar being played at the farm next door. I exited my rocking chair and softly rubbed his neck. He had a pinched nerve that had been bothering him for two weeks and I wanted to give him some relief from the pain. The dog had her head propped up on his camouflage hunting chair, lounging away as a lazy hound would. August had his legs crossed in his old chair too, and his balls were hanging down, so I rubbed those, just to make him smile. I sort of poked at them and made a whistling noise like a train.

We stayed on the porch for a little while longer and then went inside the cabin. He plopped his naked ass down on the Windsor chair and took a drink from a can of warm beer. I was sobering up a little bit, and as usual, started to drink milk. This always made me feel better after a night of intoxication—it was cold and delicious. I was feeling a little bit heavy in the heart because August let me know that he was going to take a temporary job driving a local secretary from Boston down to Georgia, and then he was going to make a delivery into the Bronx and Manhattan. It was a shipment of home brewed beer and cigarettes. I knew it was illegal but he was determined to do it. There was to be no phone contact between us, as he thought it might be listened to by the authorities, and I was to wait for him after the trip at the local truck stop in Madison, just east of Atlanta.

The no phone contact started a little earlier than I thought though, because Agnes had come back into the picture. She knew nothing of August's plans with the secretary, but she had been coming around the cabin for a few days. She was successful in running me away with her negativity and trashiness and quite successful in turning August's attitude against me. I stopped calling before he even got on the road! The depression set in, and I started to have dreams of being attacked by some person wielding a razor blade. It was ripping out my very being to be unable see August before his trip. If he could be so affected by this tyrannical woman still to this day, there was nothing I could do.

I knew that he would have sex with the secretary, but this didn't bother me at all. If his bisexuality required that he have a little pussy, who was I to stand in the way? I was a libertine after all! I wasn't going to allow my gravity to be upset by some transient law clerk. Agnes was, of course, another story all together. She had taken all of his money, taken all of his property, and stolen all of his youthful dreams. She was null and void in my book, and for God's sake, I hoped this was true for August as well.

# Must Be My Baby Coming Down

The day August was to arrive at the truck stop, I drove down there from my precious Athens. It was twenty-eight miles from the foothills to the old historic town of Madison. I had not heard from him in two weeks, and I was wondering what he was thinking, and also if he was safe, in so many ways. I didn't take the bypass around the business district, but instead drove right through the downtown and beautiful white-columned residential area. This route always made me smile and I really wanted to feel happy. When I arrived at the station, I walked through the sales area, with the hot dog stand and pornographic magazines. The truckers were coming in and out of their shower stalls, maybe having a little sexual interlude on the side. The black attendants were rushing back and forth to try to keep things on the up and up. The restroom was known to be a meeting place for horny drivers and their gay fans. I tried hard not to appear too readily homosexual and made my way to the back of the complex. There were a few illegal gambling machines in a small room so I sat down to play and tried my luck. I had a few hours to wait until August was to pull in, so it was something to occupy my time. Since this spot was near the rear entrance and showers, the truckers were milling back and forth, one after the other, and in my imagination, giving me the eye. I could see through the large plate glass window the expanse of the massive parking area. It looked like a steaming hot ocean of asphalt, their trucks slow moving cargo ships pulling into the harbor.

I waited for hours and smoked two packs of cigarettes. I would have had a few drinks but they wouldn't let me have the beer I purchased. I met a nice big Dutch truck driver, who bought me a hot dog, and we talked for a while. August knew I was there, but he never thought to call. He had the kind of mind that would often wander, and I was aware of this, so again I dismissed his lack of concern. I covered the asphalt ocean for almost twelve hours, rubbing my face, pushing up my glasses, and sweating through my jeans. I went to my friend Maria's house to sleep. It was two days later that he came rolling in.

There was only one other man, eight thousand miles away, twenty some odd years ago, and a different incarnation, that I had waited on like August. My German lover had been a dental technician, and worked at a lab in Dusseldorf. It rained constantly during the fall and winter, and I would wait outside the grey laboratory building every evening, soaked to the bone. I didn't have an automobile so I would sneak onto the streetcar without paying and lumber down Konigstrasse to the office. I had loved him in the same way I loved August. The rain fell, but I tolerated it, not really knowing if the effort was worth it, and not really knowing if they cared.

When August finally rumbled in, I knew immediately that I had lost him. Sitting next to him, perched high in the Ken-Worth cab, was a manly looking, dark-haired woman. He had met her in the parking lot of one of those gigantic general stores in North Carolina. She had been abandoned there by some ex-husband, and August offered her the ride back to Georgia. Obviously they had hit it off, because she was hovering over him and looking at me as if I were an alien. I said my greetings, and then slowly, sadly, walked across the pavement to my car. I heard the big truck start up; he had only stopped as a slight consideration.

# Hermes Scarf and Rough Woman

A few weeks after August left me, I went down to visit him. The woman had moved in with him and the dog. I met them on the front deck that night as they were grilling a steak. She couldn't keep from pulling on her long hair and twisting it around her hard face. The cabin was a wreck and all of his usual company had disappeared. When I first drove in the compound, August became pale and looked as though he had seen a ghost, and that's what I was at that point.

I cautiously walked up the few steps toward the rough woman, pulled up one of the bright, old metal chairs, and sat down. August surprisingly introduced me to his new roommate; her name was Pam. I didn't stand up and greet her as a Southerner should, but instead just stayed glued to the chair. I had dressed in an entirely black outfit, and I could see her checking me out. Ever since I was young, I had used my beautiful clothes as armor. They were always well fitted with just a slight bit of femininity to each piece. This was barely noticeable to most people. Indeed, I was there for just a bit of intimidation and had consulted Miss Pearly for the appropriate costume. She graciously allowed me to borrow one of her huge black hats with the Georgia Bulldogs "G" sewn onto the front. I also had a nice luxurious, electric blue Hermes scarf tied around my thick neck, the one that matched my silver opal ring. I realized in the moment that my tactics wouldn't take too much time to work, since she appeared on the verge of collapse from the get go.

Since I am a repository for all of my friend's secrets, I felt some kind of unearthly strength in sitting there. August was unaware of my seething temper and sadness and didn't realize that I was at a breaking point. My cup was running over with the fact that he and I had had a homosexual relationship for years, Bull and I had been intimate on several soft occasions, the oil rigger's wife wanted me to father a child for her, and Agnes was planning to smear August's reputation all over the state of West Virginia. If this woman even hinted at giving me an attitude, I was going to bust everyone's little dream world into saw dust.

I think he sensed my tension, just like when we first met on the road and had a drink at the old motel lounge. My lips, which I had inherited from Van, were pursed and the few vodka tonics had cursed what was left of my gentlemen's demeanor. I walked around the outdoor table with the huge pickle jar and drift wood arrangement to get to August's side and started to rub his legs. He made a smart-ass comment about me touching him, and Pam started to have a nervous tick, twitching her shoulders and again twisting her long hair. Somehow, her weird movements disturbed me and I felt a compassionate desperation come upon me. I had intended to dispatch her in a quick way, but she began to talk about how August was taking care of her instead of the other way around. I recognized the side effects of anti-psychotic medication with her jerking and stopped touching August. He was indeed helping her, and this was a bit of kindness I couldn't ignore. Southerners sometimes start a sentence with the words "I doubt very seriously," and I doubted very seriously that August was not only using Pam as a "beard" but also using her as a means to get rid of me. He probably thought he was garnering good karma by tolerating her. I knew they were having good sex because she had moved in, but this was too out of the ordinary for it to be real. I made a note to myself to just let it play out. Hell, this crazy bitch might really burn his house down, just like I had threatened to do for years.

# Eclipse

It seemed as though August had found his right playmate, and old Agnes was staying close to home, totally silent and totally blind in more ways than one. I secretly wished Agnes would come to her senses, regain her sight and give old Mr. Kammer a brow beating. I'm sure she wanted to, but instead she decided to pack up and actually move back to Bluefield, West Virginia, even if the packing took two years. I didn't have two years although, and the lunar eclipse was coming, something August and I had looked forward to before this woman came along.

For a couple of days, I stayed close to August's cabin. While he was working at the hardware store, I would go over and wander around the property, looking from the driveway through the trees to the open pasture where the moon would come up. I just could not get it through my thick head that he had abandoned me, but the open air helped my mind. My hometown of Athens is situated near the foothills of the Blue Ridge Mountains, and we don't have open expanses of green and sky. This lonely time at his place and the clean air had a healing effect on me. I finally got in my car and as I was driving away down the dirt road, I noticed Ashton walking naked through the edge of the hunting land next door. She looked sad too. I knew there would be no four-wheeler drive across the way, no delicious food to be eaten, no secret intimate time under the quilts, and no beautiful watermelon moon to see. I arrived back in Athens to discover that my house had been invaded again by the squirrels, and the rooms were dark as usual. I made a cup of coffee, and sat down on my favorite sofa. I covered my lap with the mink throw my Aunt Betty had given me. Then I said a prayer, and like the smoke from the bonfires at the cabin, I let his memory go.

# *About the Author*

Daniel Wesley Williams was born and raised on one of the last "old" farms in south Georgia, from which he draws much inspiration and a Southern sense of humor. He has a bachelor's degree in fashion design and resides in Athens, Georgia.